DEATH BY NAIL GUN

THE KIM MURPHY PI SERIES, BOOK #2

BY VIOLET INGRAM

DEATH BY NAIL GUN

Limitless Publishing, LLC
Kailua, HI 96734
www.limitlesspublishing.com

Formatting: Limitless Publishing

ISBN-13: 978-1-68058-699-2
ISBN-10: 1-68058-699-8

CHAPTER ONE

Bang. Bang. Bang.

I couldn't move my legs. Someone or something had a hold of my ankles. I twisted and turned, finally rolling off the bed. I opened my eyes and found myself staring up at my bedroom ceiling, my legs still entangled in the sheets.

Bang. Bang. Bang.

I freed myself and reached into the bedside table drawer where I kept protection. After brushing the condom box out of the way, I grabbed my gun, rushed down the stairs, and went out the door, nearly colliding with several of my neighbors standing on the front lawn.

Bang. Bang. Bang.

I spun and took aim.

"Oh, Kimberly, I know it's loud but you really shouldn't shoot them," said Mrs. Pelfrey.

"Oh, come on, let her wing one of them then maybe we could get some sleep," said Mr. Donnelly.

"Don't encourage her. She really shouldn't shoot

1

anyone else so soon."

Embarrassed, I put the gun down at my side. Mrs. Pelfrey was referring to the murdering kidnapper I had shot a few months ago.

My name is Kimberly Murphy, and as a private investigator, sometimes my job put me in some dangerous situations, but not today. Today was the beginning of my vacation and I wasn't planning on shooting anybody.

Bang. Bang. Bang.

Maybe.

"You'll appreciate a new roof the next time it rains," Mrs. Pelfrey said.

"I still say shoot 'em." Mr. Donnelly turned and walked off, muttering to himself.

"Don't they have to take the old one off first?" I asked.

"Oh, sweetie, you should know the old cheapskate wouldn't shell out money he didn't have to."

"Yeah, but the insurance company is paying for it because of the storm. My parents are getting a new roof on theirs."

"Well, anything that he doesn't spend on repairs goes into his pocket. That's why he told them to put the new roof on over the old one."

Now that sounded like our landlord.

"Let's just hope he didn't hire those rip-off artists or we'll all have waterbeds."

I sincerely agreed as an image of my roof collapsing on me while I slept flashed before my eyes. Back in my apartment, I went upstairs and climbed back into bed. This lasted for less than a minute when continual banging had me heading downstairs and into the kitchen. I feared with the banging of each nail going in my dream of a quiet vacation at home slipped further and further away.

My office had suffered a fire a few weeks ago, and finally, between renter's insurance and the landlord, the place was getting new carpet and a paint job, which meant goodbye, ugly wallpaper, and hello, something called Molten Sugar. I just hoped staring at it all day didn't give me food cravings. That was why I'd absolutely refused when my landlord suggested the color Chocolate Ribbon. I seriously didn't need any encouragement to eat chocolate.

New office furniture was also being delivered this week from the local Value City Furniture store. Their stuff was cheap and the delivery was free since my office was within a five-mile radius of the store. With the little bit of money leftover I was able to take the week off. That didn't mean I could fly to Rome or even Miami, but I could stay home, get some sun, and read. Plus, there would be no cheating spouses and no dead bodies. It seemed this was about as close to bliss as I could afford on my measly budget.

I made myself a breakfast that consisted of half a pot of coffee, two pieces of toast, two eggs over easy, and several slices of bacon. I sat at the dining room table, trying to ignore the racket going on above my head.

The sound of power tools had taken over my quiet suburb a couple of weeks ago. The storm chasers arrived one week after a massive storm swept through Lakeview, Ohio. No, not the fools risking life and limb to film a tornado. These storm chasers were as destructive as the storms they followed. After setting up construction and roofing companies, they went door to door convincing desperate homeowners to turn over their insurance checks. In return, those companies pocketed the money and slipped out of Lakeview, only to show up in the next unsuspecting town.

All the chaos had meant even more work for my sort-of boyfriend Detective Grant Tompkins. After months and months of denying an attraction for each other we had finally gotten down to some hot and sweaty business. He had no idea—at least I hoped not—just how long of a dry spell he'd managed to gloriously and repeatedly put an end to.

I finished eating and headed into the kitchen. In a matter of minutes I had it returned to its spotless condition. With the noise going on I was briefly tempted to go into the office, but quickly shoved the idea away. I would only be trading one set of construction noises for another. With the first day of my vacation stretched out in front of me, I had to decide what to do with it.

I ran upstairs, put on a purple bikini, and covered it with jean shorts and a white tank top. I finished it off with a pair of white sandals and a beach towel. Back in the kitchen, I made a turkey sandwich with lettuce, tomatoes, and mayonnaise. In a small cooler, I added ice, several bottles of water, and a bag of Fritos. I grabbed my purse, keys, a book, and some sunscreen and headed out the door.

Deer Creek was a manmade beach two towns

over. Twenty-something years ago the little town of Deer Creek had bought up farmland surrounding their creek. With some planning, one would hope, a hell of a lot of dynamite, and quite a bit of sand, they had created a lake with a beach. It was free, close by, and if you knew the little ins and outs, like me, you could find a secluded spot to lie out and get carcinoma, otherwise known as a yearly tan.

Twenty minutes later I was ensconced on a beach towel with a pair of sunglasses on and Jennifer Lyon's latest book. Several hours later I tore myself from the book long enough to eat lunch, then settled back in. The combination of the heat, good food, and a restless night helped me fall asleep. I awoke to gentle drops raining down on me.

By the time I packed up and ran to the car it had switched to a stinging downpour. On the way home I went through a Dairy Queen drive-thru. There was nothing better than a chocolate-vanilla swirl ice cream cone after spending the day at the beach. Back home, the rain had become a fine mist. I grabbed my stuff and headed to my patio door. Despite telling myself not to look, I did. The apartment of my now former neighbor, Lindsay, sat empty. As of last week, she had moved in with her married, soon to be divorced again, lawyer boyfriend. Rumor had it the landlord had already rented the place out again. I just wondered how long it would take for me to look at it and not think of all the awful things that happened after finding a dead body in there.

Inside, I dumped my things by the door before heading upstairs. I stripped out of my clothes and stepped into the shower. The hot water I normally reveled in hurt like hell. I looked down and shrieked. My skin resembled my ex-husband's shiny new red Mustang. It seemed I'd gotten way more sun than was prudent for a pale Irish-Italian or Italian-Irish, depending on which parent you were talking to, American girl should get. If I'd inherited my mother's darker complexion like my sister and all four of my brothers had, then this kind of thing wouldn't happen to me. I had to wonder if a lot of other unpleasantness in my life would have been avoided but I doubted it. My dad tended to avoid disasters. Unless you counted all the times he'd had to step in and help me over the years. It seemed I'd been cursed with the natural ability to get myself into all kinds of trouble while the rest of my family seemed to sail through life without so much as a hiccup. Besides skin color, I'd also been the only one to get my father's blue eyes. All of us had dark hair ranging from black to dark auburn—again, me and my dad.

I had no desire to stay in the shower and resemble someone's lobster dinner. Having experienced this several times before, I knew what I had to do. I got out of the shower and headed for the linen closet. On the top shelf was a new bottle of green aloe vera for just such a situation. I slathered it all over the front of my body before putting on some loose fitting clothes.

The rest of my afternoon and evening were spent drinking water, applying the green goo, and watching TV. The phone rang just as I thought I would go crazy if I watched one more rerun of

America's Next Top Model.

"Hello."

"Kim, thank God. I need you to meet me at my Aunt Tessa's house."

"Hey, Charmaine. What's up?"

"I don't want to tell you over the phone. Just please get your skinny white ass over here."

"Okay, I'll be there in twenty."

"Make it ten."

With that she was gone.

I ran upstairs and got dressed in a royal blue tank top, denim jeans, and a pair of sandals. I even managed to put my auburn hair up in a ponytail.

Charmaine Boudreaux and her sister, Shandra, were two of my best friends. The two shared very little in common other than DNA, a sense of loyalty, a love for family and friends, and skin that resembled the icing on a Persian donut minus the nuts. Charmaine was more interested in helping customers find the perfect knick-knack than spending her days in an office with a bunch of uptight, OCD lawyers like Shandra.

I rushed out and was in my car two minutes after hanging up the phone. Now that had to be a world record. Heck, I'd beat my own by a full minute. Maybe I'd have to check with the people at Guinness World Records. For now I drove across town, dodging cars and construction zones, arriving at Aunt Tessa's twelve minutes later. Not bad considering she lived on the opposite side of town from me. I walked up the stairs and raised my hand. Before I could knock, the door opened and I was yanked inside.

"What the hell?"

Charmaine slammed the door shut and shushed me.

"Jeez, Kim, you're late," she whispered.

"I broke every posted speed limit to get here."

"At least you're here now."

"What's going on and why are we whispering?"

"You'll see. Just follow me."

I did and passed by room after room of knick-knacks, throw pillows, and other cozy decorations that made the five-thousand-square-foot McMansion feel like a home instead of a fancy showpiece meant to impress others. We went through a pair of French doors that led to the backyard and the in-ground swimming pool. Sitting in one of the many chairs was Charmaine's Aunt Tessa. She was in her early sixties and looked like an older version of her nieces. My friend walked over and stood next to her aunt.

"Hi."

Aunt Tessa lifted her head and smiled. "Kim, I'm so sorry Charmaine called you. I told her to call the police but she refused."

"That's okay," I said, though I was beginning to think it was anything but.

Charmaine put her hand on her aunt's shoulder before looking at me. "There's a dead guy in the bushes."

"Yeah, right."

"It's true," Aunt Tessa said, reaching up and squeezing her niece's hand.

I looked at the two of them dressed in khaki shorts and t-shirts. Charmaine might play a trick on me, but Aunt Tessa would never deem such an act appropriate. "So, who is it?"

"I don't know. I've never seen that poor man before. It's such a shame too. Can you imagine, dying while you're trespassing? What is the world coming to?"

Unsure of how to answer her, I asked Charmaine to show me to their uninvited guest. She looked at Aunt Tessa, who nodded. With a final squeeze of hands, Charmaine walked toward a shed at the back of the property.

"He's in the shed?"

"Ugh, no, he's behind it."

The backyard was surrounded by a six-foot tall privacy fence. Charmaine stopped and gestured for me to go ahead. I sucked in a breath and let it out as I took two more steps and froze. Sure enough, wedged between the shed and the fence was a white man in what seemed like his thirties dressed in jeans, a white dress shirt, and black dress shoes. His head was covered with black curly hair and his eyes covered by a pair of sunglasses.

"Maybe he's not dead."

"I don't know. That's why I called you, what with you being an expert and all."

"I'm not an expert."

"Well, you've sure seen a hell of a lot more dead bodies than I have."

It was really bad when your friends considered you the unofficial expert on dead bodies, especially since she was right. Sort of.

Not wanting to disturb evidence, I walked over to a tree and grabbed a three-foot branch from underneath. I brought it back and poked the guy several times with the stick. "Hey, buddy, nap time's over."

We waited a minute and I repeated the process.

"Kim, I'm pretty sure this isn't gonna work. If it does, I'm having this bad zombie apocalypse feeling."

"Charmaine, don't ever say the word zombie when we're standing over a dead guy."

"Sorry, I don't know proper conversation etiquette for this situation like you do," she snapped.

I took the stick and gently pushed his sunglasses up. His eyes were wide open, staring, unseeing, up at the sky. "Shit." I tossed the stick toward the tree I'd gotten it from and motioned Charmaine to follow me away from the shed and the dead guy. "We have to call the police."

"Can't we just move him?"

"That's a crime. Besides, I don't really want to touch him. Do you?"

"Oh God, I didn't think about that. No way. We call the cops."

"Good. I'll stay, if you want me to."

"Hell yes, I want you to stay."

We walked toward Aunt Tessa.

"Thanks, Kim. I'm sorry I got you dragged into this," Charmaine said.

"No problem. Next time I find a body, you'll be my first call."

"Gee, thanks."

"No problem." I smiled.

We ushered Aunt Tessa into the house, got her

settled in the living room, and called the police. It really was amazing how quickly Lakeview's finest arrived at the mention of a dead body. I never understood why it was standard procedure for an ambulance and a fire truck to also respond to every call, especially since the dead guy wasn't on fire or stuck in a tree, and the only way the paramedics were going to bring the guy back was if one of them was a vampire.

I stood off to the side while Charmaine and Aunt Tessa explained how they'd gone out to water the flowers and found the man on the ground. While one of the officers stayed inside, the other went outside to check on the dead guy, taking the firefighters and the paramedics with him. I had just finished explaining my presence at the house when the other officer returned. The two had a brief whispered conversation.

Despite being the police chief's daughter and getting into my fair share of trouble, I didn't know each member of Lakeview's police force. Though lately it would seem I was meeting way too many of them. It also seemed my reputation didn't merely precede me, it entered five paces ahead of me with an entire marching band jamming to the theme from *Star Wars*.

"Miss Murphy, do you think we have time for jokes? I doubt your father would approve," said the officer who had gone outside.

"What are you talking about?"

"You know we could arrest you for this little stunt."

"Since when is reporting a dead body a crime?" I

asked.

"When there isn't a body."

Officer Snarky turned and started toward the door.

"Bullshit!"

I turned around and stormed out of the house, determined to prove the less than intelligent officer wrong. After several minutes of frantic searching, I came to the same impossible conclusion—there was no body. I stomped back into the house, brushing past the now frowning officer.

"Kim, what's going on?" Charmaine asked.

"He's gone," I replied.

"What? How's that possible?"

"I don't know."

"Ladies, it was probably just some guy who had a few too many and passed out."

"How'd he get back there?"

"Who knows, maybe he hopped the fence."

"He hopped a six-foot fence? What was he, part kangaroo?"

"I don't know what to tell you. He shows up again, give us a call."

With that, they all filed out of the house, leaving three extremely confused women behind. Charmaine was first to find her voice. "What the hell just happened?"

"I agree, but watch the language, young lady."

"Yes, Aunt Tessa."

"I'm sorry, girls, but this was quite a bit too much excitement. I'm going to go upstairs and rest for a bit."

Aunt Tessa hugged me.

"Now, I'm having the whole family for dinner Friday night. Kim, I expect to see you. Six o'clock. No excuses."

"Yes, ma'am."

"Good girl." She patted my hand and hugged Charmaine before going upstairs.

"He was dead, right?" Charmaine asked me after Aunt Tessa was out of earshot.

"Well, I sure as hell thought so. His chest didn't rise and fall. Plus, he was perfectly still," I said.

"Yeah, and what man do you know who doesn't snore?"

"None. I guess it's a good thing we're not medical examiners. We'd have been fired," I said.

"Jeez, can you imagine starting to cut him open and he pops up on the table?"

"Unfortunately, I can. That would definitely be a hell of a bad day."

"For everyone involved. Sorry I got you in this mess," Charmaine said.

"No problem. Besides, it's been three whole weeks since I've seen a dead or not so dead body, I was due."

She looked at me and we both laughed. Tears ran down my face, making me grateful I hadn't wasted time on makeup.

"Kim, do you really think it was some drunk guy or somebody playing a joke?"

"I don't know, but it makes about as much sense as anything else."

"I guess," she said, not sounding any more convinced than I felt.

"Well, unless you need me, I'm gonna head

home."

"Oh, right, yeah." Charmaine stood up, and I followed her to the front door.

"Thanks again." Before I could escape, she managed to hug me. I wasn't a big hugger, but as one of my best friends she felt entitled. After the evening she'd had, I didn't bother to fight it.

My trip home was uneventful and much closer to the posted speed limits. Suffering a severe lack of motivation, dinner was a hot dog, a bag of microwave popcorn, and a Diet Coke. My fancy meal was followed by a bag of plain M&M's for dessert. The *Legally Blonde* marathon was still going strong when my doorbell rang. Having finally learned my lesson, I checked the peephole before opening the door.

"Grant, what a surprise."

"Sorry, I've been busy. Are you going to let me in?"

It really wasn't fair. I looked bad enough to scare small children while he looked like he'd just stepped out of a magazine ad wearing a navy blue suit, gray tie with blue stripes, and dark dress shoes. To add insult to injury, there wasn't a single black hair out of place on his head.

"Sure, why not." I pushed the door open wide.

Grant stepped inside and, at six feet four, leaned way down to kiss me, but he stopped two inches from my lips, his gray eyes widened. He straightened back up.

"What happened to you?"

"A day at the beach gone bad."

"Bad? I'd say it was a lot worse than bad."

"Wow, you always know just the right thing to say, Detective Tompkins."

"Sorry." He leaned down and planted a kiss on my lips and another on my cheek. "Better?"

"A little."

"Good."

I closed the door behind him and he followed me into the living room. He took a seat in a chair facing me while I got comfy on the couch.

"So, is that," he pointed, "uh, painful?"

"Only when I touch it."

"Oh."

One look at his face and I knew just exactly why Grant had arrived at my doorstep unannounced. "I haven't seen you in a week and you expect to show up here and get laid?"

"No, I…shit." He ran his hands through his hair and damned if every single one of them didn't fall back into place. For that alone I should hate him. I watched his hands as he loosened his tie. Now that I thought about it, his reason for visiting sounded pretty damned good. I jumped up off the couch.

"Kim?"

"Upstairs. Now."

Grant and I raced up the stairs and into my bedroom. We stripped out of our clothes in record time. After his touch set my skin on fire, I sent him downstairs for the bottle of aloe vera. He smeared it over every red inch of my body, lingering over a few special places that my bikini had kept safely covered up.

After a delicate but delightful experience, we curled up and eventually fell asleep. At least until

Grant's phone so rudely began to ring at four o'clock in the morning. It seemed Grant had a dead body to deal with. Why didn't people kill each other during normal hours? Though considering my experience with Charmaine and Aunt Tessa, I was just grateful Grant hadn't mentioned it.

He got dressed in the dark and gave me a kiss before taking off. I rolled over and fell back to sleep.

CHAPTER TWO

Bang. Bang. Bang.

Shit. I groaned as the movie *Groundhog Day* came to mind. Instead of reliving an annoying holiday revolving around an extra-large rodent, I was being forced to once again listen to the less than melodious sounds coming from the roof.

The banging was back.

Resigned to the idea that my day had officially started, against my will, I climbed out of bed and walked into the bathroom. Freshly showered and dressed in a yellow tank top and jean shorts, I went downstairs to figure out what to do about breakfast.

A short time later I was seated in the dining room with an omelet and half a pot of coffee, to which I added nearly a quarter of a gallon of milk and a cup of sugar. The phone rang just as I stuffed my mouth with egg, cheese, and mushrooms. I chewed fast while grabbing the phone.

"Hello."

"Kim, how are you?"

"I'm fine, Mom. What's up?"

"What?"

I swallowed and repeated my question.

"Oh, that's better. Well, I have an appointment with the eye doctor this morning and your sister was going to take me but the little one is sick. I was wondering if you could possibly drive me. If it's too much of an inconvenience, I could always reschedule."

"No way, Mom. You've already cancelled three times."

"It's not that big of a deal. I'm fine."

"I'm sure you are. What time should I pick you up?

"Would nine thirty be okay?"

"Works for me. I'll see you soon."

"Thanks, dear. Bye."

I hung up the phone and finished my breakfast. After doing the dishes and cleaning up the kitchen I felt inspired to catch up on a few neglected chores. I folded and put away a load of towels that had been sitting in the dryer for several days before tackling the vacuuming and dusting. I finished up with the downstairs just in time to leave to pick up my mom.

When I arrived at my parents' house, my mom, dressed in a pair of tan capris, a pink blouse, and a pair of sandals, was waiting for me on the front porch.

"Hi, sweetie. Thanks for helping me out," she said after settling into the passenger seat.

"No problem."

"Are you sure I didn't pull you away from something important?"

"Not at all. Actually, you saved me from

dragging the vacuum cleaner upstairs."

"Oh, Kim, you should have told me you were busy with housework. I'd have been all too happy to reschedule."

"I bet," I muttered.

"What?"

"Nothing."

With her black shoulder-length hair pulled away from her face, my mom began to fuss with the silver hair clip.

I put the car in gear and began to back out of the driveway. "Seatbelt."

"What?"

"Your seatbelt."

"Oh, right."

It felt weird being the one giving the seatbelt reminder instead of the one receiving it. If the fiddling with the hairclip hadn't been a sure sign my mom was nervous, her forgetting her seatbelt sure was. Once she was safely strapped in, I put the car in gear and floored the gas pedal, jerking us both forward.

"Kim…"

"Sorry." I eased my foot up until, according to the speedometer, we were at least close to the speed limit.

"So how has your vacation been?"

"Fine."

"Good. You've been so busy. You need a little time off."

"Dad told you about what happened with Charmaine, didn't he?"

"What are you talking about?"

I dared a quick look at my mom's face. She didn't have a clue, which meant my dad had kept yesterday's fiasco to himself. As chief of police there had never been a chance that the nonexistent dead body situation would not have been brought to his attention. I just wondered how he'd kept my brothers quiet.

"Kim?"

"Oh, it was nothing. We just thought we'd found a dead body."

"Oh my goodness. What happened? Was it someone we know?"

"I've never seen the guy before. When a couple of dad's officers showed up, he was gone."

"I can't believe your father never said a word. I wonder why he didn't tell me."

Embarrassed, frustrated, and disgusted were the words that all too quickly came to mind. Knowing my mom wouldn't appreciate hearing my two cents' worth, I kept my mouth shut. She must have sensed my reluctance because suddenly she spent the rest of the car ride catching me up on all the goings on in our large family. I was ever so grateful when I parked in front of the eye doctor; not just because we'd reached our destination unscathed, but she had just finished up telling me about one of my uncle's colonoscopy results. It seemed my mother's nervousness over her impending eye doctor's appointment had caused her to completely forget the expression "too much information," since this wasn't the type of news my mom normally would have shared in such vivid details.

I feared I'd never again be able to sit across the

dinner table from my uncle Dante. There would be plenty of sympathy and compassion for him but none for me. Wouldn't anyone care about the trauma that knowledge had caused me? He'd been asleep, thank God, blissfully unaware. I had now endured every detail my aunt had unwisely chosen to share with my mom, who had forced this knowledge on me.

Eager to escape before she could enlighten me about any other family members and their embarrassingly private situations, I shoved the car door open before I'd even yanked the key out of the ignition. I clambered out, ignoring my mother's protests. I leaned against the car and waited. Just as I was beginning to fear I'd have to have the fire department extract my mom from the car, the passenger side door opened and she stepped out.

Inside the eye doctor's office, my mom gave her name to a blonde with purple contacts and matching mascara before choosing a seat near the door, eyeing a quick getaway I assumed. After several failed attempts to engage my mother in small talk, I leaned my head back against the wall and closed my eyes.

I had no idea how long I'd been sitting there when several gasps and an ear-shattering scream jerked me awake. I jumped out of my chair, fully prepared to pull my mom off some unsuspecting staff member. Instead of finding my mom accosting the staff, I found myself staring at two teenage boys in black shorts and hoodies. Both stood in front of the receptionist, but only one held a gun. I glanced around at the looks of terror on all the little old ladies' faces. The receptionist sat unmoving, mouth agape, staring at the teenager with the gun.

"Hurry up," he said, waving the gun around to make his point.

The other one kept his head pointed down at the floor. He never saw the old lady walk up behind him and lift her purse. He did, however, feel the smack to the back of his head.

"Ouch. Shit. Stop it."

"Don't you curse at me. Didn't your parents teach you any manners?"

The next swing of her purse hit him across the face. Meanwhile, his partner stood staring, the money he demanded momentarily forgotten.

"You have to do something," my mom whispered.

"No, I don't."

"Kimberly!"

"Crap. Fine. Call 9-1-1."

"I already did."

Looking down, I spotted the cell phone in her hand, the screen blank. Unsure if the call had gone through, I looked around. The situation was escalating, and waiting for the police seemed unwise.

Since neither of the hooded would-be bandits were looking in my direction, I stood up and walked over to the one with the gun. Realizing I'd left my guns safely locked up at home, I did the only thing I could think to do.

Putting my finger to his back, I whispered in his ear, "Hand over the gun. Now!"

"What the…?" He spun around, knocking me

backward.

"Stupid bitch. That's not a real gun."

"You're right. It's about as real as that one in your hand."

"What are you talking about? This is real," he said, pointing it at me.

I reached forward and yanked it out of his hand. "Real guns aren't made out of plastic and duct tape."

"Shit!"

He turned and shouted to his partner to run. We both looked over to where his partner was being assaulted by a group of gray-haired ladies brandishing their purses. Not waiting for his friend, he took two steps before my fist connected with his face. He grabbed my arms. Unable to shake him loose, I kicked him in the nuts. He howled in pain and the two of us tumbled to the ground. His hand grabbed my breast. For his effort, he got a left to the jaw.

"Agh, you stupid bitch."

"Stop grabbing me."

There was a bit of kicking, hitting, and swearing before I was flipped over and he was straddling me.

"Now this is better. Too bad I don't have time to give you what you need."

"Get your teeny weenie off me."

"Teeny my ass, you bitch."

He grabbed my arm. I leaned up and sunk my teeth into his flesh.

"Agh!"

"Get your filthy hands off my daughter!"

I felt a jerking motion as what I assumed was

something heavy connected with the back of his head.

I heard an all too familiar voice shouting orders and groaned.

"Mom, stop hitting him with your purse," Brandon said.

I didn't hear her response but the pummeling ceased.

"Dude, I wouldn't do that if I were you. The last guy she fought with ended up dead," Brandon said.

There was a muffled response before Brandon shouted, "Hey, stupid, get off my sister!"

"This crazy bitch is your sister? She's going to…agh. What the fuck?"

My brother, Brandon, none too gently yanked my sparring partner off me, eliciting some creative swearing.

Hopeful my embarrassment wasn't caught on someone's iPhone and posted on YouTube, I turned around and spotted several Lakeview police officers with matching stupid grins on their faces, two of which were pointing the phones at me while the third held his hand on the butt of his gun.

Brandon handcuffed the idiot and handed him off to a fellow officer.

"So, I guess staying out of trouble wasn't an option for you," Brandon said.

"Funny."

Brandon smirked before leaning down and helping me up off the floor. "Thanks."

"No problem."

"Oh, Kim, thank goodness." My mother threw her arms around me and squeezed so tightly I feared my spine would snap in half. "I'm so glad you're okay." With a final squeeze my mom released me from her Vader-like grip.

"Me too. I mean, I'm glad you're okay."

She smiled. "Of course I'm fine, dear." She turned toward Brandon. "So, do you need to take our statements or can we go home?" she asked.

"I'll send Officer Lopez over and she can take your statement. It shouldn't take long."

"What about your eye exam?" I asked.

"Oh, he couldn't possibly see patients now. I'll just have to call tomorrow and reschedule," she said.

"But, Mom, you really shouldn't put off the exam again," Brandon said.

She stared at him and I knew from personal experience that he wanted to teleport the heck out of here and away from those piercing eyes. Once my mom had decided not to do something there was no way of convincing her otherwise. Not even my dad, who carried a gun for a living, was dumb or brave enough to fight that battle.

Mom and I were just about to give our statements when Grant arrived. He said hello to my mom before pulling me off to the side. I could just tell this wasn't going to go well.

"What the hell were you thinking?"

Yep. Definitely not good. "What are you talking about?" I asked, evading his question with one of my own.

"When a couple of idiots start waving weapons around, you give them the money. You don't attack them!"

25

"Oh, so next time I'm supposed to let the jackasses beat up a bunch of little old ladies? That's pathetic."

"If only the next time was hypothetical with you." He closed his eyes and rubbed his forehead. "Next time, you will do nothing. You could have been hurt or—"

"So, does this mean you were worried about me?" I asked.

"Of course. You're related to half the department and a tenth of the fire department. Do you know how difficult that would be if they all had to take time off for your funeral?"

"Very funny. You can wipe that stupid grin off your face."

Grant looked around before taking my hand. "I was really worried. Please promise me you won't do that again." With his thumb, he rubbed circles across my wrist, sending shivers all over my body.

I gasped. "I'll try."

"I guess that's all I can ask. Now, I have to take your statement."

"Do you think that's wise?" I asked.

"Probably not, but I couldn't exactly tell your brothers I can't take your statement because I'm sleeping with you. We're all armed, and *that* would not have ended well," Grant said.

"Good point."

Grant's phone rang just as I finished up with my statement. He grabbed it and looked at the screen. "Sorry, I've gotta take this. Can I see you tonight?"

"Sure. Bring dinner."

"No problem." He turned and walked off.

I looked around for my mom and found her talking with one of the women who had been pummeling the other would-be thief with her purse. I motioned her over, and after saying our goodbyes, we got in my car and pulled out of the lot.

"I'm just so glad no one was hurt," my mom said.

"Yeah, me too. You know you're going to have to reschedule your appointment," I said.

"Of course. I'm very busy the next couple of weeks but I promise to take care of it soon."

"Uh-huh," I muttered.

"What?

"Nothing." I drove her home and dropped her off, promising to come over soon for dinner. It wasn't a difficult promise to make. My mom's cooking was incredible. Growing up in a multigenerational household, she had been immersed in Italian cuisine.

Back home, I finished cleaning, grateful my outfit wasn't accessorized by a pair of handcuffs. Then I curled up on the couch with Karin Tabke's latest book. The next time I looked up I had just enough time to get ready for dinner.

I was applying lipstick when the doorbell rang. Yay, dinner had arrived, delivered by dessert. I opened the door and for just a moment I forgot to breathe. Standing in front of me was Grant, still dressed in his navy blue suit and gray tie, only now he was carrying two brown bags of Chinese food and a six-pack of beer.

"Get in. I'm starving," I said.

"Well, hello to you too."

"Sorry." I grabbed one of the bags and led the way to the kitchen. We placed the bags and beer on the counter. I put my arms around his neck. "Hello." Grant pulled me against him, leaned down, and covered my mouth with his. Judging by the bulge in his pants, I wasn't the only one hungry for more than food. I tore my lips from his. "Upstairs. Now."

"What about the food?" he asked.

"It'll have to wait."

"Thank God."

We practically raced up the stairs and into my bedroom.

CHAPTER THREE

Sometime later we made it back downstairs and piled our plates high and grabbed a couple of beers. We ate dinner in the living room in front of the television. Sadly, it must have been a slow news day because the incident at the eye doctor's was the main attraction on the nightly news.

"Well, you made the news again," Grant said.

"Lucky me."

"At least this time they didn't have any footage of you."

"Thank God for small favors," I said.

The phone began to ring before the first commercial.

"Are you going to get that?" Grant asked.

"Nope."

"Good, because I'm kind of in the mood for dessert."

"Oh my God, did you bring chocolate?" I asked.

Grant chuckled. "I wasn't talking about that kind of dessert."

"Oh, well, I thought we had that before dinner," I

said.

"I'm thinking that was more of an appetizer. What do you think?"

"Now that you mention it, I am a bit hungry again."

"It must be the Chinese food," Grant said, standing up and holding his hand out to me. I stood up and followed him up the stairs.

Several hours later I was enjoying a deep sleep when I was rudely interrupted.

"Wake up. It's for you," Grant said.

"I don't want any."

"Kim, take it." Grant shoved the phone into my hand.

I put it to my ear and mumbled something that could have come close to hello but sounded more like, hmmmmph.

"I'm sorry it's late...Kim! Kim!" Charmaine shouted.

"Huh? What?"

"I need your help. The not-so-dead guy is back."

"That's nice. Good night," I said.

"Dang it, Kim, don't hang up on me. That dead guy is back at Aunt Tessa's," Charmaine said.

Finally the cobwebs scattered from my brain. "Oh hell," I said, sitting up.

"Exactly. I need help."

"Okay, hang up with me and call 9-1-1. I'll be there as soon as I can. And this time stay with the body," I said, swinging my legs over the side of the bed.

"Way ahead of you. I'm sitting in my car with the lights on. No way is this pale dude goin' anywhere this time."

"Tell her not to bother calling it in. I'll be there in ten," Grant said.

I looked over my shoulder and spotted Grant stuffing his arms into his shirt sleeves. I told Charmaine we were on our way and hung up.

"Go back to bed. I've got this," Grant said.

I jumped out of bed and started searching for my clothes. "No way. I promised Charmaine I'd be there. Besides, you don't know where *there* is," I said, pulling on a pair of jeans and a yellow t-shirt.

"I assume same place as the last time," Grant said.

"How do you know about that?" I asked.

"The chief's daughter and her friend call in a dead body but when officers arrive, the body's gone MIA. There's no way that stays quiet."

"The last thing I needed was my family finding out about that," I said.

"Look, I'd love to talk to you about this but I've got to get going."

"You mean *we* have to get going."

"I don't want you at my crime scene," Grant said.

"Too bad, because I promised Charmaine I'd be there." We stood, glaring at each other. "You know, the longer we stand here, the colder your crime scene gets."

Grant sighed. "Fine, but I'm in charge and you need to stay out of the way."

"Fine. You won't even know I'm there," I said.

"Yeah, right."

Thanks to the flashing lights and the fact that all

of Lakeview, Ohio's residents were safely tucked into their beds this late at night, we arrived at Aunt Tessa's house in under five minutes. Grant parked in front of the house. Charmaine jumped out of her car and ran toward us, stopping mere inches from my face. In two-inch wedge heeled sandals, Charmaine was eye to eye with me in my gym shoes. At five feet eight, it wasn't often that other women were eye level with me.

"Thank God you're here. I was about to lose it," Charmaine said.

"Where's the body?" Grant asked.

"In the bushes by the garage door," she replied.

"All right, you two stay here," Grant said.

"No problem. I've seen that dude more times than I want to," Charmaine said.

"So then you're sure it's the same guy as before?" I asked her after Grant walked off in search of the body.

"Yeah, unless it's some other white dude who decided to drop dead at my auntie's house."

"Okay, then."

"Sorry, I'm just really over this whole thing," she said.

"No problem. This is crazy. Are you okay?" I asked.

Before she could answer, Grant joined us.

"Please tell me he's still there?" Charmaine asked.

"There's definitely a dead body in the bushes," Grant replied.

"Thank God."

Grant and I looked at her.

"Oh hell, you know what I meant."

"You two get in my car and stay there. I'm going to call this in."

I sat in the driver's seat while Charmaine sat in the passenger's seat of Grant's Black Ford Fusion.

"Where's Aunt Tessa?" I asked.

"She's in Columbus visiting relatives."

"Good. She sure doesn't need to deal with this again."

"Thank God, and while I'm at it, thank *you* for being here—again," Charmaine said.

"Where else would I be? I'm just glad he's really dead this time." Charmaine looked at me. "Oh jeez, I didn't mean it like that."

"Trust me. I know what you meant," she said.

Flashing lights announced the arrival of emergency vehicles, a sight that was becoming all too familiar for me. I fought the urge to rush over and see for myself what was going on since our view was obstructed by Charmaine's car parked in the driveway.

"This time, they only brought two patrol cars, one fire truck, and one ambulance. Not bad," I said.

"Whatever. I need a distraction," Charmaine said, turning away from the house.

"Okay, I picked out a nice paint color and my cheap landlord painted it purple."

"You love purple."

"For a blouse or nail polish, not for a wall," I said.

"Sorry, Kim, but this isn't cuttin' it. I need somethin' juicy, like, say, what's goin' on with you and that divine detective out there?" Charmaine asked.

"Nothing."

"Bull. He was sleepin' over again, wasn't he?" she asked.

"So?"

"Is it gettin' serious?"

"No," I replied.

"Are you sure? That little squeak in your voice doesn't sound so sure."

"We've only been seeing each other for a few weeks." I paused. "It's comfortable."

"So what about Zack?" she asked.

Zachary Wellington was my brother Michael's best friend and my first love. Whenever we were unattached we tended to gravitate toward each other and hook up. "Nothing. We're just friends. I'm with Grant."

"Uh-huh."

There was a knock on the window, causing Charmaine and me to jump. I looked over and scowled when I saw Michael's smiling face in the passenger side window. Charmaine and I got out of the car.

"Michael Murphy, how the hell are you?" Charmaine asked.

"Terrific." He walked over and hugged her. "How are you, gorgeous?"

"I've been better."

"What are you doing here?" I asked him.

"My job. What about you?"

"I'm…"

"She's here because I called her," Charmaine said.

"Well, detective, I'd have thought you could've figured that out for yourself," I said.

"You are such a pain in the—"

"I hate to break up this family love fest but there's a dead body that needs our attention," Grant said.

"Shit," Michael said.

"Doc's on his way and the uniforms are cordoning off the front of the house. I need you to supervise the techs," Grant said.

Without another word, Michael stomped off.

"Well, that was fun," Charmaine said.

"Kim, I need to ask Ms. Boudreaux some questions. If you can promise to be quiet and not interfere, you can stay. If not, I'll give you the keys to my car and you can drive home."

"I'll behave," I said.

"Yeah, right," Grant mumbled.

"Excuse me?"

"Nothing."

Since the house was off limits, the three of us stood next to Grant's car. I stood quietly, listening as Grant questioned one of my best friends. Several times I had to bite my tongue so as not to interrupt and be sent home. Charmaine needed me to be there for moral support. That would be hard to do if I was sent home for being a bully to Grant.

"So where were you tonight?" Grant asked.

"After I closed my shop, I got ready and went out to dinner with a friend. After dinner, we went dancing."

"What did you do after that?"

"He brought me here." Charmaine cleared her

throat. "Eventually, he went home. I remembered I'd left my sweater and some paperwork in my car. When I went out to get them, that's when I found that dead guy again."

"So, he is the same man who you, your aunt, and Kim called the station about before?" Grant asked.

"I guess. Unless white folks have decided Aunt Tessa's house is the ideal place to keel over. I mean, it is hard to tell all of y'all apart."

"Charmaine!"

She sighed. "Look, I'm sorry. It's been a long day. Yes, it's the same dead guy as before. Only this time he didn't get up and go anywhere."

"Where is Aunt...I mean, Mrs. Boudreaux?" Grant asked.

"She's visitin' relatives in Columbus," Charmaine replied.

"So, besides the other day, have you seen that man before?"

"Nope. I've seen that man twice and that was two times too many."

Grant then began questioning us both about our previous encounter with the dead guy. We had just finished up when the coroner, Dr. Ralph Gardner, arrived.

I had never been any good at following orders— a main reason I wasn't on the police force. So I ignored Grant's instructions to stay put while he talked to Dr. Gardner. I told Charmaine to hang out by the car, then made my way up the driveway. I did my best to hear what they were saying, but other than an occasional word, my eavesdropping attempt was a giant failure.

Undeterred, I took several more steps until I was only a couple of feet away from Grant's back.

"For now, all I can confirm is he's dead. As to TOD, the liver temp suggests at least forty-eight hours. The COD will have to wait until I get him back to the morgue. I assure you, detective, as soon as I know more, so will you."

"Thanks, doc," Grant said.

"Kimberly, what a lovely surprise. How are you dear?" Doc Gardner asked.

"Better than that guy," I replied, ignoring the daggers in Grant's eyes.

"Yes, well, I should hope so," the doctor said.

"Doc, the dead guy," Grant said.

"Yes, yes. Goodbye, dear. Hope to see you soon." He cleared his throat. "Alive and well, of course, not on one of my tables." With that, he sauntered off to collect the body.

Grant closed his hand around my upper arm and not so gently guided me back down the driveway.

"What did I tell you about disturbing a crime scene?" he asked.

"Well, I'd think this is more of a body dump than the actual crime scene. Plus, while the uniforms are putting up all that yellow tape, they might want to think about wrapping up the backyard as well," I said.

"Damn it!" Grant spun around and stomped up the driveway.

"Good Lord, that man is hot. Even when he's all angry and whatnot," Charmaine said.

"That was not my fault. Oh, wipe that stupid grin off your face."

37

"Oh please, that man has it bad for you. I almost feel sorry for him," Charmaine said.

"Hey, is the front door open?" I asked.

"Yes. Why?"

"Good. Stay here." I took off before she could ask me any more questions. No one stopped me on my way to the front of the house. I wasn't stopped when I opened the door and went inside. I made it to the back of the house without being questioned. I opened the patio door and was about to step outside when a shadowy figure blocked my path.

"You just can't help yourself, can you?" Grant asked.

I stifled a scream and clapped my hand to my chest. "Jesus, you scared me half to death."

"Well, it's a good thing Doc Gardner's still here."

"Very funny," I said.

"What are you doing back here?"

"I just wanted to make sure you knew where the body was the last time."

"I read the report. We're all good," Grant said.

"I just thought that since I was here before, I could be of some help."

He sighed. "Fine. Just watch your step."

Grant followed me over to the shed. I explained to him what happened and about poking the man with a stick.

"Funny, I haven't heard that part of the story before."

"Well, I didn't feel it was important."

Grant laughed. "I'll bet. Now, you need to leave and take Charmaine with you." He handed me his keys.

"What about you?" I asked.

"I'll catch a ride with one of the units."

"Okay, well, thanks."

"No problem. Just do me a favor." He ran his hand through his brown hair. "Stay out of trouble. Please."

"I'll do my best."

"Shit." Grant turned and walked toward a small group of officers.

I returned to the car and found a crowd of gawkers that included several local TV reporters. The bane of my existence, Mr. Abraham, saw me and started walking toward me. I raced over to Charmaine. "Get in the car. Hurry," I said, then jumped into the driver's seat of Grant's car and locked the doors as soon as we were both inside.

"Lord, Kim, you about gave me a heart attack," Charmaine said.

"Sorry, but we've gotta get out of here." I started the car and pulled away from the curb. I watched in part horror, part gratification as Mr. Abraham jumped out of the way to avoid the front bumper. "Awesome."

"Where exactly are we going in such a rush that you damned near took that man out?" Charmaine asked.

"That was that stupid reporter who keeps sticking his dumb camera and microphone in my face."

"Oh, well, why didn't you say so? I'm sure you'd have only gotten a few points on your license if you'd nicked him."

"Okay, so, where do you want to spend the night? I can take you home or you can crash at my place."

"I really don't want to be alone at my place."

"No problem."

We drove the short distance in silence. At my apartment, I parked Grant's car in the back lot, next to my car. We entered my apartment through the patio door. Since Charmaine had spent the night at my place before, she knew where everything was. I sent her upstairs while I headed for the kitchen. I made a desperate search for something chocolate. Anything would do. Luckily, in the door of the refrigerator, I found a piece of Esther Price candy.

Thanking God, fate, and karma, I grabbed it and bit into it as if it was the last piece of chocolate in the world. I locked up and climbed the stairs to my room. Once there, I stripped out of my clothes then pulled a pink nightshirt over my head before crawling under the covers.

CHAPTER FOUR

For the first time in days I didn't wake to the banging sounds of the roofers. Instead, my unwanted early morning wake up was to the sound of raised voices. I briefly considered hiding under the covers and going back to sleep. The thought that one of my neighbors could call the police had me climbing out of bed and following the yelling until I was standing in my living room looking at Charmaine and Shandra in the middle of a verbal battle that would not end well for any of us if I didn't stop them.

"Not that I don't enjoy getting up to the joyous sounds of a good argument, but seriously, what the hell?"

"Oh, Kim, I'm so sorry. We'll keep it down. Go back to bed," Shandra said.

"Well, you should be sorry for coming over here and yellin' at me," Charmaine said.

"What is wrong now?" I asked.

"Ask her. She's the one who started it," Charmaine said.

"Do you have any idea how embarrassing it is to be called into your boss' office and asked about your family's involvement in a murder investigation?" Shandra asked.

"Nope. I'm the boss, and I don't give myself crap over stuff like that," Charmaine replied.

I was also my own boss but I still got yanked in and questioned about this kind of stuff all the time. It did, however, make me think about what it must be like for my dad and brothers.

I was the youngest of six kids. My four older brothers were all cops while my sister got married right after college graduation and became the family baby factory. That was supposed to be my own fate, and would have been if I hadn't caught my husband having sex with someone else. In hindsight, the jackass had done me a favor, but I'd spend eternity in Hell before I admitted that.

"Look, I get it. We should have called you, but you needed the whole deniability thing. You knew nothing about it and it shouldn't affect your job," I said.

"I don't care about my job. I mean, I do, but family and friends are always a priority. You know that."

"Of course we do. We were just trying to keep the collateral damage to a minimum," I said.

"Exactly. You should be thanking us," Charmaine said.

Shandra glared at her sister. I cleared my throat.

"What?" Charmaine asked.

"Don't push it," I muttered.

"Fine. Whatever. I'm hungry."

42

Now that Charmaine mentioned it, so was I. "Charmaine, you get the coffee started and I'll get breakfast. How does Bob Evans sound?" I asked.

"Like Heaven."

I looked at Shandra. "Are you hungry?"

"No. Besides, I've got to get back to work."

"All right, give me a second to get dressed and I'll walk you out." I turned to go and stopped. "No fighting while I'm gone."

I walked out of the room but not before I heard Charmaine mutter, "Okay. Okay."

I ran upstairs and into my bedroom. I stuffed my head and arms through a purple t-shirt then slipped on a pair of white shorts. In the bathroom, I washed my face and ran a brush through my hair. When it wouldn't cooperate I tied it all back in a ponytail holder and raced back down the stairs. Charmaine and Shandra were just where I'd left them, doing their best to ignore each other. At least they weren't trying to kill one another so I considered it a slight improvement.

"Okay, Shandra, let's go." I grabbed my purse and followed Shandra out the back door. "Look, I know we should have called you—again. We were just trying to protect you," I said.

"Kim, I don't need protection." Shandra frowned.

I knew she could be tough when she needed to be but this mess could cost her a job. No way would any of us risk that. "On this one we're just going to have to be on opposite sides."

She opened her car door. "You know, it drives you crazy when your family does this to you."

"That's different," I said.

"How?"

"Because, besides a smart mouth, I also carry around a Glock."

"Kim!"

I rolled my eyes and promised to call her first if anything else happened. What Shandra didn't notice was my fingers crossed behind my back. I protected those I loved, and if that required the occasional lie, so be it. Considering my track record, I was surprised when Shandra didn't ask to see my hands. Maybe she was maturing faster than the rest of us. That made me a little sad—for her. Sigh.

Fifteen minutes later I stepped back inside my apartment and was greeted with the glorious scent of fresh brewed coffee. Charmaine and I took everything into the dining room and enjoyed some of Bob's sausage gravy and biscuits, home fries, and scrambled eggs. After dumping enough milk and sugar into the coffee to make it drinkable, we sat in silence and ate. When we were finished I tossed the empty containers into the trash and stuck the mugs in the sink.

Charmaine said she needed to get home so she could get ready for work. I dropped her off and before she got out of the car she told me that my mom had called and invited everyone to dinner tonight. It seemed she wasn't taking no for an answer from any of us. I told Charmaine I'd see her tonight and drove off. With no particular plans, I considered going home and crawling back under the covers. While it held a great amount of appeal, it wouldn't be any use. I was pretty sure the roofers would be finishing up today and sleep would not be an option.

So instead I drove to the grocery store and loaded up on the necessities: milk, bread, coffee, donuts, bologna, *People* magazine, nail polish, and a giant bag of M&M's. I was waiting in line when a group of teenagers kept pointing at me and whispering. Fearing my face had a sudden bout of acne, I grabbed a mirror out of my purse and checked for the evil dots from Hell. Finding nothing amiss, I looked over at the group of people that would one day be running our country and frowned. Annoyed with their laughter and pointing, I shouted, "What is so damned funny?" In return the little gray-haired lady behind me gasped.

"You're the lady from YouTube," one of the kids said, pointing at me.

"What are you talking about?" I asked.

In response, the kid stuck his cell phone in my face. There on the tiny screen was the eye doctor's waiting room. Oh crap. There I was in all my glory brawling with the idiot would-be robber. Well, shit.

"Isn't it awesome? It already has, like, twenty thousand views," he said.

"Swell." I couldn't believe that many people had seen me wrestling on the ground with the idiot. I so did not need that kind of publicity. I finished checking out and rushed outside to my car.

Back home, I put the groceries away and was just about to find out the latest gossip on Johnny Depp when the doorbell rang. With regret, I placed the magazine down on the coffee table then opened the door. To my horror, local reporter Mr. Abraham was standing in front of me.

"Sorry, I get my news on the Internet." I tried to close the door but he put his foot in the doorway. "You'd better move that foot unless you want to lose it."

"Now, Miss Murphy, is that any way to talk to someone who can make you famous?"

"I don't want to be famous. I want to live my life and be left alone by creeps like you," I said.

"Oh, come on. Everybody wants to be famous and I can give you that. All you have to do is give me an exclusive."

"You are insane. Now, if you don't remove your foot, I'll remove it for you." He must have believed me because he yanked his foot out of the way. "Goodbye, Mr. Abraham. I so hope I don't ever see you again." With that I slammed the door and locked it.

Hoping for no more interruptions, I sat down in the living room to read the magazine. Halfway through I was bored and decided to call my cousin Jackie and see how she was doing. The fact that she worked at the police station and had access to all the dirt had absolutely nothing to do with my sudden need to check in with her. However, if she did let something slip about the body that disappeared, I certainly wouldn't deprive her of the opportunity to share that information with me.

"Kim, what's going on? I heard your office is getting a purple makeover," Jackie said.

"The paint was on sale."

"Now I appreciate a good sale as much as the next girl, but really, that's a bit extreme."

46

I couldn't agree more but it wasn't my choice. I was, however, going to have to look at it each and every day. It had me wondering if I'd be doing a lot more work at home.

"So, any news on the body Charmaine found?" I asked.

"Oh boy, is there."

"Like what?" I asked.

"Crap. Detective Delicious is on his way over. I'll call you when he's gone," Jackie said before hanging up.

Just great. I hated the thought of waiting but I didn't have much of a choice. It wasn't like Grant would tell me anything. This was his case and my friend and I were involved. Not directly of course, but enough that my asking questions could look like a cover-up or worse, like the two of us were guilty.

The sensible thing to do was to wait for Jackie to call me back. Grant was a busy man. How long could he possibly take standing there talking? After ten minutes I was slightly frustrated. At fifteen I was annoyed, and at twenty I was angry and unreasonably jealous. I really didn't want to think about that. At twenty-five minutes I grabbed my phone to call Jackie when it rang in my hand.

"Hello."

"Sorry about that. Good Lord, it got busy in here. I mean, don't these people realize I've got things to do. I can't spend all day talking. By the way, Michael said to tell you not to be late to dinner."

"I won't be, but why is he so concerned whether I'm late or not?" I asked.

"I have no idea, but knowing your brother, he's

probably just worried about his stomach."

Maybe, but whatever it was it was going to have to be a worry for later. For now, I had a problem with a dead body. "So, what did you find out about the dead guy?" I asked.

"Check your email. I think you'll find something interesting in there," Jackie said.

"Oh, thanks, Jackie. I owe you."

"Don't I know it. Actually, just don't get caught doing something illegal and we'll call it even."

"You got it."

I said goodbye before heading upstairs. In my home office, which was really a bedroom minus the bed with a desk, chair, and some file cabinets, I turned on the laptop and checked my email. Ooh, I had a Groupon for frozen yogurt, but that would have to be for later.

I opened the email and printed it out. The dead man's name was Derek Patterson. According to his driver's license he was thirty-five years old and lived in Oakwood, Ohio, an affluent town just south of Dayton. He was much cuter in his photo than he'd been in person. I wasn't sure what that meant considering how awful ID photos were and the only times I'd seen him he'd been dead.

The next few pages were a copy of Dr. Gardner's autopsy report. According to Lakeview's friendly medical examiner, Mr. Patterson had the misfortune of having four nails, each one almost two inches long, imbedded in his heart. Ouch. Not a pleasant way to go. There were worse ways, but this wouldn't make my list of favorite ways to make my exit from this world.

Personally, I was hoping that one evening when I was extremely old, I'd fall asleep and just drift up to Heaven. Well, if I was going in that direction. If not, I'd pass on the whole dying thing.

I went through the rest of the report and didn't learn anything that seemed important enough about the man who someone shot four roofing nails into his heart. That took a lot of anger.

Mr. Patterson didn't have a police record, and hell, the man didn't even have a single traffic ticket in the last ten years. Yup. Something was definitely off about the guy.

Seeing nothing else of importance I tossed the report on my desk. On the off chance I'd find something I googled Derek Patterson. Unfortunately, there were over six million entries. There was an artist, a hockey player, a football player, and a musician all on the first page. Of course none of these were the Derek Patterson I was looking for. Adding Ohio to the search led me to a funeral home and a million other entries.

Frustrated, I shut off the computer and took the report with me downstairs. I curled up on the couch and tried to think about what I should do. The sensible thing to do was to leave it alone and let Grant figure it out. Since this wasn't my case and Charmaine and I weren't suspects, dropping it was exactly what I would do. I closed my eyes while I decided what I would do with the rest of my day.

The doorbell rang. I got up to answer it and then my phone started playing the theme song to *Scooby-Doo*. I chose to ignore my phone and opened the door. Charmaine was on my front porch, all four-

49

by-four feet of it. She brushed past me and I closed the door behind her.

"You will not believe what that man of yours is up to!" Charmaine shouted.

"What?" I asked.

"Detective Tompkins is at Aunt Tessa's house questioning her."

"About what?"

"The dead guy, what else?" Charmaine said.

"Oh right, of course." I shook my head in embarrassment. "So, if he's there, what are you doing here?"

"They kicked me out."

"They?"

"Aunt Tessa and Detective Tompkins. Can you believe that? They acted like I was interferin'."

I could believe it but thought it wise not to mention that. "Did Aunt Tessa have a lawyer with her?" I asked.

"No."

"Shit." I knew Grant wouldn't cross a line when questioning her, but I didn't like this. "Call her. Tell her not to say another word until we get there."

"Damn it. I knew I shouldn't have left." Charmaine grabbed her cell phone while I went for my purse and keys.

"Don't bother," Charmaine said when I returned.

"What do you mean?"

"He left already. Now, is that a good thing or a bad thing? 'Cause the look on your face makes me think Aunt Tessa's in a whole lot of trouble," Charmaine said.

"I'm sure everything is fine." I plastered a smile

on my face and did a silent prayer that I was right.

"I hope so. I'd hate to think of what I'd do to that man if he upset my aunt," Charmaine said.

"Why don't we wait and see what happened before you need me to raise bail money for you," I said.

"Fine. I'm gonna run back over to Aunt Tessa's before I get ready for dinner."

"That sounds like a great idea," I said.

Charmaine opened the door. "I'll see you at your folks' house. Melissa crawled out of her writing cave long enough to text me that she'll be there tonight. Of course Shandra will be there too. Wonder what all the fuss is about."

"I have no idea. In all honesty I've been trying not to think about it," I said.

"No need to worry. This is your family we're talking about. The only one who gets into any real trouble is well…you."

"Thanks."

"Sorry, the truth sucks."

We said goodbye and I closed the door behind her. Charmaine was right. I was the family troublemaker. Not on purpose. I just tended to find myself in some unusual situations. It wasn't like I went out looking for them. *Liar*, said the little voice in my head. Okay. Maybe. Sometimes. Whatever.

I went back to the living room and checked my cell phone. I'd missed two calls. The first one was from Melissa confirming she'd be at Chez Murphy tonight. The second was from Grant asking me to call him back. I did but my call went right to his voice mail. I left a message that I was returning his

51

call and hung up.

I picked up the report on Mr. Patterson. Derek owned a roofing company. Well, after all the storms we'd had recently his business must have been doing well. Insurance companies were forking out tons of money in claims. Not that I felt sorry for them because come January they'd all be raising their rates.

Mr. Patterson was married to a Shaina Geiszler-Patterson. According to the papers she was a full-time wife and part owner in her husband's company. The couple had been married for six years and did not have any kids. There was a note that warned they did, however, have five Chinese Crested dogs. One of which had peed on his shoe and another had tried to bite him when the detective, Grant, had gone to make the death notification.

I tried my best not to laugh but oh Lord that was funny. Poor Grant. I'd have to remember to be more careful. No, actually, I wouldn't, because I had no business going over there. Determined to let the matter drop I took the report upstairs and stuffed it in one of the desk drawers.

***

I pulled into my parents' already crowded driveway with five minutes to spare. Dinner was usually served promptly at six o'clock. Heaven help the person who arrived late. Not only would you endure my mother's wrath but, worse, you would possibly miss out on her delicious food. It didn't seem to matter how much extra she prepared, it all disappeared. Rare was the occasion that my parents had leftovers.

The smells of spices that I could only guess at met me at the front door. Tempted to head straight for the kitchen, I ignored my grumbling stomach and followed the sounds of laughter into the family room. All of the people I loved most in the world were in there. Oddly, instead of filling every available seat, they were all standing around in the center of the room. My brother Brandon was the first to notice me.

"Kim! Hey, everybody, Kim's here."

Every head turned toward me. This wasn't good. "I'm not late so what's the deal?"

"Nothing," Brandon said.

"Aunt Kim, you were so funny," said my nephew Logan.

"What are you talking about?" I asked despite the unsettling feeling I knew exactly what they, my loving family, had been watching.

"You're a star," my niece Erin said, running over and hugging me.

"Oh great. That damned video," I said, sending Erin into a fit of giggles.

"Language, young lady," my dad's voice boomed.

"Sorry."

"It was awesome when you elbowed that guy in the face," Logan said.

"That was cool, but I liked it when she took him to the ground," Michael said.

"You've gotten, like, half a million views," Erin

said, smiling up at me.

I looked around the room and most of my loved ones had the good sense to avert their eyes or cover their mouths in an attempt to hide their smiles. Of course my brothers were openly laughing and making sarcastic comments.

"I'm so glad I could be everyone's pre-dinner entertainment." I spun around and headed for the door.

"Kimberly, stop right there."

I turned around and found my mom frowning. Just great. Here came the lecture.

"I am thoroughly disappointed in you."

"Mom, I'm—"

"Not only was Kimberly responsible for stopping an attempted robbery, thanks to her, those two hooligans the department has been trying to catch for months are now safely behind bars," Mom said.

I felt my mouth drop open. While I searched for the ability to speak, my family had the decency to apologize.

"It was just dumb luck," Michael muttered. "We would have gotten them. The idiots robbed the eye doctor's thinking no one would be able to pick them out of a lineup."

"That may be, but Kim should be credited with the arrest," my mother insisted.

Michael opened his mouth, I assumed to disagree, but one look at our mother's disapproving face kept him quiet.

"Now, if everyone could head to the dining room, it is time to eat. Kimberly, dear, I could use your help in the kitchen."

Not a single person believed my mom needed any help, especially mine, but no one said a word. I said a silent prayer and followed her into the kitchen.

"Thanks, Mom," I said.

"For what?"

"For defending me. I'm sure that wasn't easy."

"I know they were being difficult but they love you," she said as she started handing me oven mitts and dishes of food to take to the table. "They just want what's best for you. Even if they don't always know how to show it."

"Uh-huh," was my witty response.

"It's true," she said.

"I guess." I shifted the casserole dish. "Mom, did you mean it about those idiots?"

"Isn't that wonderful?" She smiled. "I'm just so glad those two young men are off the street. Now, let's go eat."

After my dad said grace, the family got down to the important task of making my mom's salad, garlic bread, fried calamari, eggplant parmesan, and lobster ravioli in tomato cream sauce disappear. Gianna Murphy had surely spent all day in the kitchen preparing this meal for our family. I looked around the room and frowned. With so many people stuffing their faces I held little hope there would be any left for me to take home for tomorrow's lunch.

I didn't know if it was bad luck, karma, or fate that had me stuck in the seat next to Zachary Wellington. I'd always had a weakness for his black hair and brown eyes. The damn thing was he knew it and used it to his advantage. I'd given him my virginity when I'd been a senior in high school and he'd been a worldly college junior. Zack and I had also fallen into the habit of hooking up when we were both unattached. Thankfully for both our sakes, especially Zack's, the men in my family were none the wiser about our sexcapades. At this point I was almost positive my mom had her suspicions, but she never asked and I never told.

With such a large group to feed, my parents had taken my mother's inheritance and had a house built to their specifications. An extra-large kitchen and a dining room large enough to accommodate a formal dinner at the state capitol in Columbus were must-haves. It turned out a pool and a man cave had also been deemed necessities.

Despite plenty of room, Zack's leg somehow kept rubbing against mine. Each time it sent a wave of lust straight to all my girly parts. One look at him and it was obvious he was enjoying my discomfort. I briefly considered giving him a dose of his own medicine but knew it would certainly not go unnoticed, as we were surrounded by five highly observant police officers.

So instead, I placed the heel of my shoe on top of his foot. I only used a minimum amount of pressure but it was enough for Zack to shift his leg from mine. Ah, success.

The rest of the meal was peaceful, at least for me. None of what passed as witty banter was directed at or about me so I relaxed. Before dessert was served, my sister, Brenna, announced that she was expecting twins. I shouted *yes* the loudest, earning some confused looks.

While everyone else jumped up to hug and congratulate my sister and brother-in-law, Zack leaned over and whispered in my ear. "Takes some of the pressure off of you, doesn't it?" He chuckled.

"Yes, it does. Too bad your sister isn't a baby factory." I smiled.

Zack frowned. "I wish. I love her, but if it meant getting my dad off my back, I'd be thrilled to be Uncle Zack again."

"So not interested in any little Zacks running around?"

He leaned forward and placed his hand on my thigh. I sucked in a breath as heat radiated throughout my whole body. "Depends on who's asking. I might just be willing to take you up on that offer," he whispered.

"You are going straight to Hell. You know that, right?"

"That's okay because I'm pretty sure you'll be joining me." His hand squeezed my thigh before moving toward my…

"Don't." I gasped, jumping up. If not for Zack's quick save the chair would have landed on the floor.

Zack chuckled. "You're only delaying the inevitable."

"Just keep telling yourself that," I said before walking off to congratulate my sister.

The rest of the evening I did my best to avoid being alone or too close to Zack. He had the uncanny ability to make me forget all the reasons why we shouldn't be together.

I had my escape all planned out. As soon as my sister and her brood got up to leave, I'd wait five minutes before I headed for home and freedom. I didn't have long to wait. Everyone was saying their goodbyes to my sister when phones began to ring.

I pulled mine from my purse and panicked at the caller ID. It was the police station number. "Hello."

"You are not going to believe this," Jackie said by way of greeting.

"What's wrong?" I looked around the room and watched as Michael shouted into his phone, "Is he insane?"

"Hello?"

"Huh, sorry. What did you say?" I asked.

"Detective Tompkins made an arrest for that dead body you and Charmaine called in."

"That's great. Isn't it?" I said, feeling uneasy.

"Yeah, well, normally I'd agree, but not this time."

"Why? Who'd he arrest?"

"Crap. Hang on a sec."

I tapped my fingers on the end table while I waited.

"Okay. Sorry about that. Detective Tompkins arrested Charmaine's aunt for the murder," Jackie said.

"He what?"

"Uh-huh. Can you believe it?" she asked.

"Look, Jackie, I gotta go. I'll call you later." I hung up and looked around the room. It seemed everyone without a phone glued to their ears suspected something as they sat anxiously looking around the room.

I zeroed in on Charmaine and Shandra, who were sitting next to each other. They needed to know. I stood up and froze. I wasn't sure how to tell them.

"Thank you, everyone, for a wonderful evening, but I'm afraid we're going to have to call it a night," my dad said. The remaining guests began to say their goodbyes. "Ladies, I need you to wait here."

Charmaine, Shandra, Melissa, and I took seats and sat quietly until my parents returned to the room. They were followed by my brothers Michael and Brandon.

"I'm sorry to have to be the one to tell you this but earlier this evening, one of my detectives made an arrest. Charmaine and Shandra, your Aunt Tessa has been arrested for murder."

"What?" Shandra asked.

"That's insane!" Charmaine shouted. She stood up and put her hands on her hips.

"There's no way," Melissa said.

"Now, I've already spoken with Charles about representing her."

Charmaine started to say something but my dad held up his hand.

"Tessa's bail hearing is set for tomorrow morning. Charles will do his best to get her out on bail."

"She has to spend the night in jail?" Charmaine asked.

"I'm afraid so. Michael has talked to the guards. They'll be making sure she's okay," my dad said.

My dad patiently answered all the questions he could. Eventually, exhausted and out of questions, there were hugs all around and promises to meet at the courthouse in the morning.

Back home, I climbed the stairs and got ready for

bed. I set the alarm before crawling under the covers.

CHAPTER FIVE

The next morning the alarm went off. My first inclination was to shoot it. Instead I hit the snooze button before I remembered why exactly I'd set it during my staycation. I climbed out of bed and jumped into the shower. After drying my hair and putting on makeup, I briefly considered my regular attire of jeans and a t-shirt. Since I was pretty sure my mom would go crazy if I showed up in court dressed like that, I stood in front of my closet and pondered my options. Sadly, the options weren't as vast as I would have liked.

I glanced at the clock and frowned. I had promised to get to the courthouse early. To keep that promise I had exactly seven minutes before I had to leave. I grabbed a little black dress that wasn't too tight or too short and black one-inch heels.

I got in my car and sort of obeyed the speed limit. I parked in the lot and made my way through security, thankful I'd had the good sense to leave my guns at home. Well, except for the one I'd been keeping locked in the trunk of my car, under the spare tire.

After enduring the elevator ride for four horrendous floors, I got out and started walking toward the last courtroom on the left. I heard my name and looked around. Standing in a hallway on the right was Grant.

"I figured you'd be here sooner or later." Grant leaned against the wall. "Your whole family, well, almost all of it, is waiting down the hall."

"Of course I'm here. I still can't believe you arrested Aunt Tessa."

"Look, I was doing my job," Grant said, folding his arms.

"I understand that, but you're wrong. She's innocent," I said.

"The evidence points to her. What else was I supposed to do?"

I couldn't believe how stubborn he was being. Why couldn't he see what was right in front of his face? "Sometimes the evidence is wrong."

"This isn't the movies or a TV show. People don't get set up."

"Really? Because it happened to me," I said.

"Yes, it did, but that's because weird and crazy are pretty standard for you."

"Wow. Thanks." My face was on fire, from embarrassment or anger I wasn't sure.

"I'm sorry, Kim, but it's true," Grant said.

"It may be, but only a jerk would say it." I spun around and found Zack standing only a few feet away. Just great. The embarrassment would never end. I started to walk away.

62

"Kim, wait," Grant said.

I didn't bother to look back. I just kept walking. As I passed Zack, he fell in step beside me.

"What was that about?" Zack asked.

"I don't want to talk about it," I said through gritted teeth.

"No problem."

He placed his hand on my arm. I turned my head toward him.

"Are you okay?"

"I'm fine."

Zack smirked. "I'd say you're a hell of a lot more than just fine."

For once I didn't rise to the bait and did my best to ignore the little flutter in my stomach his comment caused. He opened his mouth but then closed it as we were suddenly surrounded by friends and family, preventing him from blurting out whatever it was he'd been about to say.

It wasn't long before we were ushered into the courtroom. While we sat in the pew-like seating for observing, Zack and his dad walked up front and took the seats for the defense lawyers. The judge entered the room and everyone got quiet. As I sat listening I did my best to ignore Grant sitting on the side of the room behind the prosecutor.

After a bunch of back and forth between the defense and the prosecutor, the judge finally announced that he was setting Aunt Tessa's bail at one million dollars. The prosecutor looked annoyed as he'd been arguing against bail in a murder case. Normally, I'd have to agree with him, but not this time. Aunt Tessa was innocent, and since I couldn't count on Grant to find evidence clearing her, it was going to be up to me.

Eventually everyone left, but Shandra, Charmaine, Melissa, Zack, and I stayed behind. Zack was quick to assure everyone Aunt Tessa would be fine while she waited for her bail to be posted. He recommended a bail bondsman located only a few blocks away. Shandra and Charmaine thanked him and asked if I'd go with them, but Zack asked me to stay behind for a few minutes. I agreed and told my friends I'd meet them at the bail bonds office in a few minutes.

"It's bad, isn't it?" I asked.

"I'll be honest. It doesn't look great."

"What can I do?"

"I figured you'd want to help. I want to hire you to investigate. Later today the prosecutor will be turning over the evidence he has. I figured you could go over it tonight."

"Of course, but I'm volunteering my services."

"I thought you'd say that, and so did Aunt Tessa. She's informed me if you don't treat the case like any other, I'm to hire someone else." He smiled. "She's a stubborn woman."

"Fine. Whatever. We'll work out the details later," I said.

"Good. Do you need a ride to the bonds office?"

"No, but thanks."

The two of us just stood there as if neither of us was willing to walk away. Zack reached over and tucked a loose strand of hair behind my ear. His fingertips brushed against my skin, sending little electric sparks down the side of my face.

"I have to go." I backed away from him.

Zack dropped his hand to his side. "I'll call you later when the files are ready."

"Okay. Great." I spun around and headed off, trying not to think about the hurt I'd seen in his brown eyes.

At the bail bonds office, I arrived just in time to learn that Aunt Tessa would be released in a couple of hours. I offered to go to the jail and wait with them but Charmaine and Shandra assured me they would be fine and that they'd call if they needed anything.

After hugs all around, we said our goodbyes and parted ways. Having skipped breakfast, I was starving. I walked to my car and headed for the nearest McDonald's drive-thru. I ordered a Big Mac Value Meal and a large Diet Coke. I had just pulled up to the window to pay when my cell phone rang. I dug the phone out of my purse and handed it to the confused woman with gray hair, too much blue eye shadow, and bright red lipstick.

"Oops. Sorry." I took the phone back and handed her a five dollar bill.

I said hello into the phone and nodded my thanks to the woman when she handed me my change and a receipt. I froze for a second when I heard my office landlord, Paul Rodgers, say my name. After the purple paint debacle I cringed in fear at the thought of what else could have possibly gone wrong. Sadly, I had an extremely vivid imagination.

"Kim, I need you to get over here right away," Mr. Rodgers said.

"Oh jeez, what's wrong now?" I asked, pulling

up to the next window. "Sorry, what was that? Who is dead?" I asked just as a teenage boy with way too many piercings in his face handed me my drink.

Mr. Rodgers explained that a woman had shown up at my office desperate to hire me. "She said something about her husband and a slutty redhead from his office. Her words, not mine," he stressed. "Then she started crying. I don't know if she said he was dead or is going to be. Either way, I need you to get over here and take care of her."

"Look, I'll get rid of her for you, but you're gonna have to wait. I'm in the middle of a lunch appointment." I reached over to get the rest of my order and found the guy staring at me. I smiled but the guy tossed the bag at me and closed the window. Weird.

"Miss Murphy, I have been married for thirty years to a wonderful woman but there is one thing I can't handle and it's a woman crying. For the love of God, please help me."

"Fine, but I'm downtown. It'll take me about fifteen minutes to get there," I said.

"Fine." He sighed. "Just hurry." He hung up as I drove out of the McDonald's parking lot.

Thirteen minutes later I arrived at my office. I brought the empty food wrappers inside and tossed them in the trash. I walked around and found Mr. Rogers sitting at the reception desk and a brunette sitting in one of the waiting chairs.

Mr. Rogers smiled and jumped up out of the seat when he saw me. "Oh good. You're finally here." He ran a hand through his gray hair. "Miss Murphy, this is…"

A woman near my age of twenty-eight, with gorgeous brown hair down to her waist, stood up and walked over toward me. She extended her hand. "Hello, I'm Mrs. Thornton. Your landlord has been kindly keeping me entertained while I waited."

"Hello." I shook her hand and suggested we go inside my office for some privacy. Sadly, Mr. Rogers explained that the furniture hadn't arrived yet. So unless we wanted to sit on the floor, we'd have to do business in the waiting area. He said his goodbyes and rushed out the door. I only wished I could have gone with him.

"So, Mrs. Thornton, what can I do for you?" I pointed to the seat she'd vacated then sat in the chair behind the reception desk.

"Well, Miss Murphy, my father is in poor health. My husband and I have hired around the clock care for him. I've been happy with the care he's received but lately one of the young women seems a bit nervous around me. I don't understand why. I haven't mistreated her or been rude or disrespectful in any way."

"Okay...so, what is it you'd like me to do?" I asked.

"I want to have hidden surveillance cameras installed inside my home." She brushed imaginary lint off of her cream colored silk blouse. "My husband and I will be gone for two days. The house will be empty tomorrow from nine in the morning until about six at night. I was hoping that would give you enough time to get done." She looked at me and smiled.

I was never surprised anymore by just how

quickly the rich expected the rest of us to get a job done for them. It didn't matter if they'd thought about it for weeks, once they made up their minds it was hurry up and get it done time.

"Tomorrow? That's kind of short notice," I said, calculating just how much time and equipment I might need. The Thornton house had been highlighted in a magazine a few years ago. I remembered my sister going on and on about how the house boasted eight bedrooms and nine bathrooms in just over ten thousand square feet.

"Yes. I'm afraid the trip came up last minute and this will be the only time the house is empty." She quoted me a number that was triple what I would have suggested. At that point it was a no-brainer. I grabbed a contract and she and I signed it. She left with her copy after giving me a check for half as a down payment. She also gave me the information to get into her house without setting off any alarms, plus her specific instructions on where she wanted the cameras installed. She stared at me for a moment. I guessed she was looking for judgment on my face. If that was the case, she wouldn't be seeing any. I figured that my home, or in my case, apartment, was my sacred place. If anyone was inside taking care of a loved one, they'd damned well better be taking the most excellent care; because if they weren't, I'd be sending some work Dr. Gardner's way.

It was odd that she wasn't interested in using the alarm company they already had in place for outside. Maybe she suspected the nanny cams would pick up something she didn't want those without a signed non-disclosure agreement to see. Whatever, their loss was my windfall.

This job was going to be too big to handle on my own. I needed reinforcements. Fortunately for me, I had plenty of people to choose from. I knew my brother Michael would help but he'd spend the whole time complaining about who put me in charge. My twin brothers, Justin and Jason, would be far too busy after putting in full shifts with the SWAT team. They had families of their own that needed and wanted their attention. Brandon was the best solution to my problem. He'd complain while he worked but he'd get the bulk of the job done and he wouldn't hassle me over the legality of nanny cams.

I left a message on his voice mail asking him to call me about a job. I checked in with my landlord before heading out to the nearest branch of my bank to deposit the check. My next stop was back downtown. There was the perfect shop for people in my line of business. It was also helpful for those people who were either paranoid or just had an expensive hobby.

After struggling with parallel parking, I went inside and headed straight for the back of the store and the owner, Max Santiago. Max was retired military. He'd served in Afghanistan, Iraq, and a few other nasty places before a piece of shrapnel all too close to his spine put an end to his career in the Marines.

After he left the military he was desperate for something to do. He tried several private security firms but quickly got fed up with all the bullshit.

Next he took the night shift at a local gas station. He lasted there six whole months until the night some little punk stuck a gun in his face. Max had subdued the would-be robber and called 911. In return for his bravery he'd been fired for going against store policy.

The owner of Smith and Sons' Cameras admired Max's gumption and hired him as the store's new manager. Eight years later, Mr. Smith, who had no heirs, left the business to Max.

"Kim Murphy, my favorite customer. I just love it when I see your smiling face." Max was sitting behind a desk wearing a *Star Wars* t-shirt. His gray hair was pulled back into a ponytail almost as long as mine.

"You just love my credit card and how you get to gouge me."

He laughed. "There is that. What can I do for you today? I've got some really cool drone cameras."

"Thanks, but that's a bit too flashy for what my client needs."

"Ah, so subtle is what you need." Max rubbed his right hand across his chin, revealing scars on the back of his hand.

I filled him in on what I needed. He assured me he'd have everything ready to go in about half an hour. I walked the four doors down to the bookstore. As was my usual habit, I headed for the mystery section first. After picking six books I walked to the front of the store in search of the romance books.

I was just about to reach for Sylvia Day's newest

release when I glanced at the clock above the giant fireplace and was surprised to discover I'd been in the bookstore for an hour and a half. I rushed up front to the register, paid for my books, and headed for Max's shop.

"There you are. I was afraid I'd have to send out a search party for you," Max said.

"Sorry. I got distracted."

"I noticed." He glanced down at the bag in my hands.

"I can't help it. Books and chocolate are my two guilty pleasures," I said.

"Funny, I'd have guessed sex was your number one." Max laughed.

It was hard to pretend to be indignant when that really was one of my top three. "So, how much do I owe you?" I asked.

Max quoted me a price that made me flinch. My client may be rich but I wasn't. We haggled back and forth for a bit until we came to an agreement on a price we could both live with. I paid with a credit card and Max helped me carry everything out to my car and put it in my trunk. We said our goodbyes and I headed home.

I parked in my reserved spot and took several trips to bring all of the stuff inside. I had debated leaving the equipment locked up in the trunk of my car but considering how expensive that stuff was it wasn't worth the risk. As penance for skipping the gym that morning, I decided to torture myself by dragging all the surveillance equipment upstairs and into my home office.

When I was finished I headed back downstairs

and straight into the kitchen. I opened the refrigerator and freezer doors and stood there wishing that somehow a plate of my mom's antipasto and veal scaloppini would magically appear. When that didn't happen, I contemplated the wisdom of eating an entire pint of mint chocolate chip ice cream. I had just decided it was acceptable when the doorbell rang. With regret I closed the doors and headed to see just who was interrupting my dinner.

I looked through the peephole and sighed. One of my greatest temptations was just on the other side of the door and it was being delivered by a man I always had trouble saying no to. I never stood a chance and he knew it. Damn him. I opened the door and Zack smiled.

"Are you going to let me in? These are heavy," Zack said.

"What are you doing here?" I asked, doing my best to ignore the heavenly scents emanating from the bags.

"I told you I'd bring you the files. I just figured we could work and eat."

I inhaled the food and groaned. Zack laughed as I stepped aside to let him in.

"I knew you couldn't resist."

"Don't be smug. The only reason I let you in is because you brought food and I'm starving," I said.

"Sure. Whatever you have to tell yourself."

I closed the door and followed him into the dining room. I wasn't surprised when Zack brought out containers of all my favorites—wonton soup, crab Rangoon, garlic chicken, beef with vegetables, shrimp fried rice, egg rolls, and pot stickers. The man knew my tastes, and not just in food, all too well.

"It was all I could do not to dive in on the way over." Zack took a bite out of an egg roll and offered it to me. Despite the little voice in my head screaming at me not to encourage him, other parts were ready to go.

"I'll go get plates." I grabbed the food from his hand and rushed out of the dining room. I thought I heard him laugh but could have been mistaken. In the kitchen, I finished off the egg roll and got plates and silverware. Next I stood in front of the refrigerator and debated the beverage choices. There were several bottles of Coors Lite beer left and a bottle of cabernet sauvignon. Since we were supposed to be working I chose to forgo the alcohol for a couple of cans of Diet Coke.

I took everything back into the dining room and tried not to smile when Zack, upon seeing the cans of diet pop, raised his right eyebrow. "Sorry, I haven't made it to the store. It was either this or orange juice," I lied.

"Diet Coke it is," he said.

We piled our plates high and dug in. "So, where are the files?" I asked.

"In my car. I didn't want the food to get cold. Plus, I'm starving. I was running late and had to skip breakfast so I could make it to the gym this morning and be to court on time. Then lunch was two bites of a roast beef sandwich and an onion ring."

Zack was a distraction I didn't need. I figured

that the two of us could work together and be professional. I'd been dealing with my attraction to Zack since I was a pre-teen. What were a few more hours in the grand scheme of things? Besides, Aunt Tessa needed us.

There were so many reasons why having sex with him would be wrong. At least until I figured out what was going on with Grant and me. Suddenly I realized Zack was ignoring his food and staring at me. "What?"

"If you keep looking at me like that and licking your lips, I'm gonna take you right here on this table," he said.

"Don't. We can't." I put my hand out as if to stop him.

"Are you sure?" he asked.

I was contemplating an answer when the doorbell rang. I jumped up and ran to the door, eager to delay that conversation. I yanked open the door and felt my mouth drop open to find Grant standing there. It took several attempts before I stammered out hello.

"We need to talk," he said.

"Okay. About what?"

"This case. I know you don't agree with what I did but..." He stopped talking and glared at me.

I looked around and spotted Zack standing a few feet behind me eating a pot sticker. Grant eyed me up and down, which, under other circumstances, would have led to pleasant activities, but not this time. "I see you're busy." He turned and started walking toward the street and his car.

I ran after him. "Wait a minute." I grabbed onto

his muscular arm.

He stopped walking and turned around. "What?"

"Why did you just leave?" I asked.

"I was obviously interrupting something." He pointed back toward my apartment.

"Zack is an old friend, and he's Aunt Tessa's lawyer. We're working on her case."

"Working over dinner, huh? Kim, I'm not an idiot. I've seen the way he looks at you, but worse, I've seen the way you look at him." He pulled his arm away from me.

"Grant, Zack is practically family." Grant clenched his fists. I didn't think he'd use them on me, but I took a few steps back.

"I can't deal with this bullshit. You can do whatever the hell you want!" He turned and stormed off. This time I didn't try to stop him. I walked back inside and shut the door. Zack didn't say anything as we walked toward the dining room. Instead of following him, I veered off and headed straight for the refrigerator. I grabbed the bottle of wine and two glasses.

"Are you okay?" Zack asked, pointing to the wine.

"Just freaking great."

Zack placed the food containers, plastic forks, chopsticks, and napkins on the table. He must have sensed my frustration at numerous failed attempts to open the bottle. He gently took the wine from me and successfully opened it on his first try. Zack smiled and poured wine into both glasses. He set the wine bottle down and handed me a glass and picked up the other one for himself.

"To better days," he said, raising his glass in the air.

"I'll drink to that," I said before gulping down half the yummy liquid in my glass.

"You might want to slow down," Zack said.

"Not in my nature."

"I know." He smiled and finished off his glass.

I reached for the bottle and refilled both of our glasses. Soon the bottle and the glasses were empty again. Zack went into the kitchen and returned shortly with a six-pack of beer, the last remaining alcohol in my apartment if you didn't count the mouthwash in my bathroom.

"I'm not so sure that's a good idea," I said.

"That's too bad because I was thinking we could finish these off upstairs."

Zack smiled and I groaned. Damn him. He knew I had a weakness for that smile of his. One day it would most assuredly lead to my downfall. Until then, I guessed I'd just have to enjoy it.

"Let's finish them now and then head upstairs."

"Deal."

I woke up with an arm across my chest. I took inventory and realized it wasn't my arm. I turned my head and sighed. Lying next to me was a completely naked Zack. There was no light peeking in through the window. I looked at the alarm clock next to my bed. It was two o'clock. Damn. I was having a hard time remembering much past Zack and me finishing off the bottle of wine and then finishing off the beers.

Some of the events were starting to come back to me, in extremely vivid detail. Oh wow. My little life would be so less complicated if I could blame my actions on the large amount of alcohol I'd consumed, but I couldn't. I had to be honest, at least with myself. Zack was my first true love. Well, if you didn't count the jerky boy in kindergarten who broke my heart by acting as if I didn't exist.

It seemed that no matter what I always found myself drawn back to Zack. He was the reason I'd gotten married so young. Why I'd overlooked my ex-husband's numerous flaws. I was afraid. Afraid of my feelings for Zack. Afraid of getting hurt when he stomped on my heart.

I'd still managed to get hurt. I'd caught my lowlife ex running his tongue all over our slutty neighbor. I hadn't seen it at the time but that had been a blessing. Otherwise I'd have had kids with that lying piece of scum and been tied to him forever through our kids.

Suddenly I didn't feel so good. Even though I was a hundred and fifty percent sure Grant had dumped me, the least I could have done was wait more than a few measly hours before I had sex with someone else.

I slid Zack's arm off of me and climbed out of bed. I went downstairs and grabbed a glass of water and two Tylenol. Hopefully this would prevent too much suffering in the morning. I put the empty glass in the sink and went back upstairs. I crawled under the covers and had just gotten comfortable when Zack's hands began to roam.

"Go back to sleep," I said.

"I'll sleep later." His right hand cupped my breast and I had trouble remembering all the reasons the two of us were a bad idea.

The little voice in my head whispered something about guilt and I told it to shut up. As Zack yanked the covers off me and pulled me against his erection I decided to go for it. I mean, we'd already done the deed, and I might as well get as much enjoyment out of the rest of the night as possible.

CHAPTER SIX

It was ten thirty when I pried my eyes open. I felt the other side of the bed but it was empty except for a piece of paper on the other pillow. According to the note, Zack had left the files for Aunt Tessa's case on my desk. He'd headed home early to get ready for work and would see me later. And just like that the joy of a night of fantastic sex was replaced with unease. I cared about Grant a lot. Was it love? Not yet, but the sex was terrific. We got along, as long as we weren't arguing over his job or mine. Most other topics had been safe except that he was a Cleveland Browns fan and I was a Cincinnati Bengals fan.

One more look at the clock had me jumping out of bed with no apparent side effects from last night's overindulging. I ran downstairs and got a pot of coffee started before heading back upstairs, into the bathroom, and taking a shower.

After drying off and putting on purple matching bra and panties, I covered my underwear with a pair of white shorts and a purple tank top. Downstairs, I downed two cups of coffee after adding half a cup of sugar and half a pint of milk.

Not interested in anything I had in the fridge, I filled a travel mug with even more coffee before making several trips to secure the equipment back into the trunk of my car. When I was done I grabbed my purse and cell phone then locked up my apartment. I turned on the car and was blasted with hot air. While I waited for the oven-like temperature to cool down, I called Brandon.

"Kim, I was just about to leave. What's up?" Brandon asked.

"Bill's Donuts or McDonald's?" I asked.

"Both. Just kidding. Donuts sound awesome."

"Cool. I need some help." I filled him in on what I needed and gave him the address.

"No problem. I'll see you there," Brandon said.

"Great. Thanks," I said.

I drove the two minutes to the world's best donut shop that was conveniently located in my neighborhood. Inside, I was grateful to have missed the morning rush. The line was short and I was back out in under five minutes.

I drove to Mrs. Thornton's house and found Brandon and his pickup truck waiting for me. I pulled into the drive and punched in the security code and the gate swung open. I zipped through so that Brandon would have enough time to get through. The homes in this part of town started at five thousand square feet and sat on at a minimum of three acres. The long, winding driveway curved and revealed the enormous house that had been hidden from view.

I parked in front of the behemoth and got out of my car. Brandon pulled up and parked next to mine. I popped the trunk and waited for Brandon to help.

"Wow. This place is huge," Brandon said.

"This is going to take a while."

"Luckily we have all day. Did she give you the security codes?"

"Yes. We should be all set," I said.

"Good. I'm starving."

My stomach growled and reminded me I hadn't eaten anything yet either. I grabbed the donuts and coffee and the two of us leaned against the hood of my car. I gave Brandon the coffee I'd bought him at the donut shop and grabbed mine. We stood there and devoured breakfast in silence.

The silence was nice. No pressure. It was one of the things I loved about Brandon. Even when he was angry he tended to hold back, mull the situation over before discussing it or, in many cases, explaining to me, rather loudly, how stupid and dangerous something I'd done had been. It was also one of the things that made him a great cop and a pretty damned good brother.

"What?" Brandon asked.

"Nothing."

"You had that weird look on your face."

"I was thinking."

"Normally, I'd say don't do that, but in your case, I'm grateful."

"Ha-ha." I stood up and grabbed my trash. "Are you done?"

"Yup," he said, stuffing the last piece of donut in his mouth.

81

We cleaned up and decided to do a walk-through before bringing the equipment inside. I closed the trunk and locked the car. We walked up to the main entrance and I started feeling uncomfortable.

"Why do I feel uneasy?" Brandon asked.

"Because it kind of feels like we're breaking and entering. Well, except for the breaking part," I said.

"And just how would you know?" He put up his hand. "Wait. Don't answer that. I sure as hell would hate to have to testify against my baby sister."

"You know, you missed your true calling. You should have been a stand-up comic."

"No way. I wouldn't get to carry a gun. Besides, the ladies love a man in uniform."

"Oh, please stop before I throw up," I said.

"Okay, then. Stop stalling and let's get this over with."

Of course I'd been stalling but I was surprised Brandon had known what I was up to. I took a deep breath and grabbed the key and the note with the code from my pocket. I tried to ignore my shaking hand. If Brandon noticed, he was kind enough not to say anything. I stuck the key in the lock and turned. The door opened. I rushed inside, found the keypad, and was about to punch in the security code.

Brandon grabbed my arm. Confused, I turned to look at him. He put his finger to his mouth. "Alarm's off," he whispered.

I looked back at the display. He was right. "Shit."

"Go out front and wait for me."

"No way. I'm not leaving you in here."

"Kim, I'm the cop, you're the civilian. Go outside. You hear anything, call 9-1-1."

"But…"

Brandon pulled a gun from under his shirt. "Go!" he hissed.

I rushed outside but there was no way I was leaving him alone without backup. I raced to my car and grabbed my gun and cell phone. I ran back inside and began searching the rooms on the first floor. The downside to a house that size was burglars could be hiding anywhere. It could take hours for just the two of us to search every square inch and every possible hiding place. This was stupid and dangerous. I debated calling for help but fear for Brandon's safety won out over my fear of embarrassment. I called Michael and said a silent prayer of thanks when he answered his phone.

"Look, I was hired to do inside surveillance. I got here and the alarm was already turned off. I need help."

"Get the hell out of the house and call for the patrol officers."

"I would but Brandon is already inside." I didn't think it prudent to confess my own current location.

"Goddammit, Kim!"

"I'm sorry. Please just get here."

"I'm out the door. Text me the address and don't do anything else stupid." Michael hung up and so did I before stuffing the phone in my pocket.

I kept my gun out and kept moving forward. As I got to each door, I opened it and did a cursory search. Seeing no one and nothing obviously out of place, I kept going. I had just finished the first floor when I spotted Brandon in the kitchen, his gun down at his side. I walked forward and must have made a sound because Brandon spun around and pointed his gun at me.

"Damn it, Kim, I could have shot you!" He put the gun back down to his side.

I would have made a smart-ass comment but for the real fear I saw in his eyes. "Sorry. Have you searched the second floor?"

"No, not yet. I spotted a couple in the hot tub. I was debating going upstairs to see if they had friends with them before confronting these two."

"Okay. You confront those two; I'll go upstairs and search." I moved to go past him but Brandon grabbed my arm.

"No way. I'm the cop. You get those idiots. They're naked and less likely to have weapons on them." He turned and headed for the stairs.

"Why don't you wait? Michael's—"

"No time to wait." With that he was up the stairs and out of sight.

I sighed that his reasoning made sense but I still feared for his safety and prayed Michael would get here fast. I checked my gun to make sure it was loaded and the safety was off. I turned the doorknob and pulled the door open. Thankfully it didn't squeak. I stepped outside and walked toward the couple in the hot tub. As I got closer the sounds of their activity reached my ears.

"Oh, baby, keep going. Don't stop. You know I like it when you do that."

The donuts I'd hungrily scarfed down weren't sitting so well in my stomach anymore. Damn. Just as I was about to step around a rose bush and announce myself, I froze. I was conflicted. First, what was I going to say? I wasn't a cop. I couldn't yell, "Freeze. Police." So what the hell was I going to say? Plus, shouldn't I at least wait until they had concluded their business? While I debated, they solved the second half of the problem for me by concluding their interlude. With that hurdle out of the way I jumped out and yelled freeze.

I found myself staring at two ancient and naked individuals. Oh great. I'd just caught the oldest gatecrashers on the planet. Where were the witnesses with their cell phones all too eager to post this on YouTube with my other notorious adventures? The woman gasped, ran over, and grabbed a towel from a patio chair. She covered herself up while the man started shouting.

"Who the hell are you?" the man demanded. I thought he'd also duck for cover but the man showed no interest in covering his dangly bits or any other parts. Seriously, why couldn't he have had the good sense to get back in the water to cover his rapidly deflating sword?

"I'm a private investigator and you two are trespassing," I said once I got the urge to laugh under control.

"Bullshit. This is my home." He pointed to his chest while I did my best to avoid looking below the bellybutton.

"I see you've got this all under control," Brandon said.

"Very funny," I replied.

"Freeze. Police!"

Just when I thought it couldn't possibly get any worse. All hell broke loose. Over the next twenty minutes there was a whole lot of shouting and carrying on but eventually the confusion was cleared up. It seemed I had walked in on my client's father and his caregiver having sex. The two were in love and wanted to get married but he hadn't wanted to hurt his daughter's feelings and her memory of her late mother. Turned out it was kind of difficult to look your boss in the eye when you knew you were doing her dad behind her back.

Two patrol officers, Michael, Brandon, and I walked out the front door. It was hard to tell who was the most shocked. Though, if I was placing bets, I'd say I was the most embarrassed. We had barely made it to the cars when everyone busted out laughing.

As I feared, it didn't take long for the jokes to be directed my way until one of them went just a tad too far.

"So, Kim, if you wanted to see a man naked, all you had to do is call." Officer Bello laughed.

And just like that, all teasing stopped. Michael and Brandon sent both officers rushing for their patrol cars with identical looks of fear on their faces.

"Finally. Thanks for the support," I said.

"Hey, no one makes fun of our sister but us," Brandon said.

"That's right. Plus, there's no way I was going to put up with him hitting on my baby sister in front of me. Where was the respect? What an asshole," Michael said.

"First of all, I'm not a baby, and second, it had nothing to do with you." I turned and attempted to stomp off, but Brandon had me stopping dead in my tracks.

"Yeah, besides, aren't you already dating someone?"

It was just dumb luck I was facing away from them. Otherwise my shocked expression—mouth open, bugged eyes, and red face—would have sold me out faster than my niece for a chocolate chip cookie.

"No, I'm not," I said, which was technically true.

"Weren't you dating—?"

"I've gotta go."

Once safely ensconced in my car, my sigh of relief morphed into laughter, which halfway home contorted into tears. By the time I arrived home I was openly sobbing. Inside my apartment, I headed straight for the couch and grabbed a blanket and allowed myself to wallow in my own guilt.

I had no one to blame for the mess I was in but myself. This sucked. I considered for a moment if a Reese Witherspoon marathon was necessary but decided what I really needed to do was dig into Aunt Tessa's case. I went upstairs and after a stop in the bathroom to wash my face, I went into my home office, sat at my desk, and began to read.

The dead man, Derek Patterson, must have really pissed off someone. I mean, they were angry enough to put four roofing nails in the man's chest. I'd been angry at people plenty of times, but dang, even I wouldn't do that to someone.

One thing I was sure of, Aunt Tessa didn't kill

this guy. Charmaine, maybe, but she'd have had the good sense to call the cops and there would have been a good reason—like she was protecting someone. I could see her using a baseball bat, but a nail gun? Nope. Which meant someone else had. Plus, that same person had moved the body not once but twice.

A few hours later I came up for air. I needed a break. I also needed to clear my mind for a bit before jumping back in and taking notes. Downstairs in the kitchen, I made a turkey sandwich with lettuce, tomato, mayonnaise, and two pieces of bacon. I cut it in half and grabbed a Diet Coke and a handful of Fritos.

I was torn between going back upstairs and reading or watching TV while I ate. I used to watch *Days of Our Lives* with my grandmother but it had been a while since I'd watched it. A quick glance at the clock and I realized I'd already missed it for the day. Well, damn. How was I supposed to find out what was up with Hope?

I flipped on the TV and tried to enjoy the distraction while I ate. It didn't work so I gave up and took the rest of my lunch upstairs to my office. I grabbed a notebook and pen and started jotting down notes. The next time I looked up it was six o'clock. My stomach growled with the unnecessary reminder that it was dinner time.

I went downstairs and into the kitchen. Despite my intent to ignore the answering machine I couldn't resist the flashing number. I was a bit surprised to see I'd missed ten calls while I'd been ensconced in my office. Jeez. I sat down and pressed play. I picked up a pen and notebook that I kept next to the phone to take notes. It soon became apparent that that wouldn't be necessary. The annoying reporter, Mr. Abraham, had left three messages. For a supposedly smart man, he sure didn't learn. I would never help him. Ever.

I had also missed two calls from Charmaine and Shandra, plus one call from Melissa. The rest were for a lawn service, a satellite company, and someone interested in selling me a home security system. I had my own version of home security—a Glock.

I was torn between returning my friends' calls and making dinner. Another growl from my stomach made the decision for me. Honestly, I was grateful for the delay. I'd spent hours going over Aunt Tessa's files and, well, it didn't look so great. It could have been far worse, like, say, a confession, but it could have been better with an airtight alibi.

After a search of the kitchen I decided on a grilled cheese sandwich, a bowl of chicken noodle soup, and the rest of the Fritos. This time there was no urge to retreat to my office. I took my dinner into the living room and sat down on the couch. I picked up the remote and began flipping through the channels. I found a repeat episode of *Treehouse Masters*. I loved that show. The treehouses were so awesome. I wanted one but I was pretty sure my apartment landlord wouldn't let me, even if I could afford one. Sigh.

After dinner, I cleaned the dishes and tidied up the kitchen. When I felt I couldn't stall any longer I went upstairs and dug my cell phone out of the bottom of my purse. One quick glance and I frowned. I had also somehow managed to miss several calls on my cell phone. It was time. No more stalling. I punched in the phone number and held my breath.

"Kim, I was just thinking about you," Zack said.

I ignored, or at least pretended to, the shiver that ran down my spine at hearing him say my name. "The case against Aunt Tessa…it's bad."

"Yes, it is. That's why she needs us. Look, I'm just about to wrap things up here at the office. Why don't I come over and we can go over everything? I'll bring dinner."

"Sorry, but I've got plans," I lied. "I've made a list of people I want to talk to."

"Good. Possible suspects?" he asked.

"We'll see. I'll email you the list. I'll get working on it in the morning," I said.

"That's fine. Are you sure you don't want me to come over?" he asked.

It was all I could do not to give in to temptation, but somehow I found the strength to resist. "I'm sure. Ooh, that's Melissa calling. Gotta go. Bye," I lied before hanging up.

I sighed and leaned back against the couch. What the heck was wrong with me? I was a grown woman. I should be able to have a normal relationship. Yet somehow I just couldn't handle it.

I loved Zack. I always had, and I feared I always would, but we were just too different. He was designer suits, fancy dinner parties with champagne, and expensive sports cars, while I was jeans with a t-shirt, fast food takeout with a beer chaser, and I was just grateful if my current car could be counted on to make a round trip. For me, cars were a necessary evil since you were either stuck making car payments or car repairs.

On paper, Grant and I were probably better suited for each other. He was casual clothes, when not in suits for work. Grant hated fancy restaurants and long lines. For vehicles he was more pickup truck than foreign sports car.

At least Zack had the good sense to be a Cincinnati fan, both football and baseball.

I shook my head. None of this mattered right now. I had priorities and my love life would have to take a number and get in line. I picked up my cell phone and called Charmaine. We agreed to meet at Aunt Tessa's house at nine in the morning. She assured me she'd pass on the message to Shandra.

Next I called Melissa and left a message. It was evening so I figured she had locked herself in her writing cave, otherwise known as her gorgeous office with shelves and shelves of books, a fireplace, a saltwater aquarium, and a view of a small pond.

The view from my real office was of the parking lot and the dumpster. My home office was a little better with a view of the park located behind my apartment building. That is if you looked past the building with the bathrooms.

With the rest of the evening stretched out in front of me, I wasn't sure what to do. I glanced down at my nails and decided it was well past time for a manicure. I would have chosen the color that best fit my mood but they didn't have anything named

Frustrated, Confused, and Exhausted. I settled on something the bottle called Vividly Violet. I just loved the way it looked in the light.

I was hoping the pretty purple would cheer me up. It didn't. I thought about the list of names I'd jotted down. It was a long list of people to speak with but it had to be done. I just hoped the killer's name was on the list. I'd love nothing better than to wrap this case up real fast so Aunt Tessa could get her life back to normal.

I was letting the second coat dry when my cell phone rang. I looked at the screen and groaned.

"Hello, Mrs. Thornton. How are you this evening?" I asked without really wanting to know the answer.

"Not very well, Miss Murphy."

I was right. I hadn't wanted the answer. "Sorry to hear that. What can I do for you?"

"My father is insisting that you come over here. He's refusing to talk to me without you."

"What?" Of all the things she could have possibly said, this was the weirdest. "That doesn't make any sense."

"No, it doesn't, but that is the situation. So, if you could please come over here right away so this matter can be resolved."

I tried to think of an excuse to get out of it but didn't think she'd accept I was waiting for my nails to dry. When nothing came to mind I assured her I would be there soon. I hung up and ran upstairs to run a brush through my hair and apply some lipstick and mascara.

With my purse and my keys in hand I went

downstairs and out the back door. In the car, I wondered if I should call Brandon. After a moment I decided it would be best not to include him. The last thing I needed was to drag him into whatever disaster I was about to walk into.

I arrived at Mrs. Thornton's and pressed the button. Someone must have been waiting for me because I'd barely brought my arm back in the car when the gate started swinging open. Oh goody. I pulled up to the front of the house and parked. The thought that maybe I should enter through the servant's entrance had me stiffening my spine and lifting my head. No way in hell was I going to let some rich people intimidate me.

I walked up the steps and briefly wished I was facing down an armed burglar as opposed to the very irate family I was about to have to face. I raised my hand to knock on the door but it opened before I could.

Mrs. Thornton was standing there, full makeup, not a single strand of brunette hair out of place. Her skin, paler than my own, was covered in a dress so white it looked like a sheet of notebook paper.

"Miss Murphy, come in." Mrs. Thornton stood aside so I could enter.

The look on her face had me rethinking my decision to leave my gun in the car. "Thanks." She closed the door behind me and I followed her down the long white hall. I looked and felt out of place among all the expensive designer touches. It was funny. I hadn't thought about that earlier when I'd been walking down this hall, gun in hand, searching for my brother and intruders.

Mrs. Thornton led me into a room where her father and his girlfriend slash caretaker were seated on an overstuffed sofa. A gentleman I recognized from photos in the paper and around the house as Mr. Thornton, my client's husband, stood across from them. He was dressed in a dark suit and tie. His brown hair, cut in a typical executive cut, was graying at the temples. There was just a hint of wrinkles on his face while his wife's skin was flawless.

"Thank God you're here. Maybe now we can get some answers," Mr. Thornton said.

Well, it was nice to know someone was happy to see me. Since a quick scan of the faces in the room seemed to indicate I wasn't extremely popular and they could all do without my presence. "So, what can I do for you?" I asked before I could chicken out.

"You can start by explaining to me why you didn't install the surveillance system. Plus, why is it that my father is refusing to speak to me about what happened today in *my* house?"

"You wanted cameras in the house? What were you thinking?" Mr. Thornton asked.

"I'll tell you what she was thinking. She sent this woman to spy on me," Mrs. Thornton's dad said.

"I'll do whatever I have to do to ensure my family's safety," she said, then turned back toward me. "Well, I'm waiting for an answer."

I took a deep breath and slowly let it out. "I came to the house today to install the nanny cams and things, like we discussed, but when I got here the alarm system was turned off. I found your father and this woman…" I pointed to the lady sitting next to Mrs. Thornton's father, "…in the hot tub. They were, um…"

"They were what?" she asked.

"Having sex."

"Oh my God." Mrs. Thornton spun around. "Dad, how could you?"

"Now, dear, Gretchen and I love each other. I didn't want you to find out like this," he said, waving his hands around, "but we're getting married."

"Like hell you are," Mrs. Thornton said.

"Honey, maybe you should calm down," Mr. Thornton said.

His wife spun around and stared at him. "Calm down? My father wants to get married." She turned back toward her father, who was holding hands with Gretchen and whispering what I assumed were comforting words to her. "Absolutely not."

Her father patted Gretchen's hand before standing up. "Now, listen here, young lady. I'm a grown man and I will not take orders from you or anyone. I'm getting married and if you don't like it, then Gretchen and I will get our things and leave. Tonight."

"You try leaving this house with that woman and I'll call the police."

"You need to watch that tone. I will not take orders from you."

"Oh yes, you will. I'll not have you shaming our family or Mother's memory by letting you marry a member of the staff," Mrs. Thornton snapped.

I sucked in a breath. Oh jeez. This was crazy

personal but I couldn't make myself stop staring. My head bobbed back and forth like I was glued to a tennis match. I wondered if I should leave, but then I wouldn't get to see how this all played out.

"Don't you dare speak about Gretchen like that. Your mother is gone. She would want me to be happy."

"How do you know?" Mrs. Thornton asked.

"Your mother and I were married for forty years. Did you honestly think we never discussed this?"

"I guess. I don't know."

"Sweetie, when your mother got sick she made me promise I wouldn't spend the rest of my life sad and alone. I made her make me the same promise."

"I guess that makes sense, but what about one of the lovely women from the country club?"

I tried but the laugh refused to be silenced. Everyone in the room turned and looked at me. I think they had actually forgotten I was in the room—until now. "Sorry."

"No, please, go ahead. I'm glad you're finding my family's situation amusing," Mrs. Thornton said

I got a great deal of business thanks to referrals so I had always done my best not to piss off clients. Since I had already screwed this up, referrals wouldn't be winging my way anyway, so I figured what the hell. "Mrs. Thornton, I assume you want your father to be happy. I also assume that before you hired Gretchen, you had her checked out—a background check, drug testing."

"Well, of course."

"Then if she was good enough to work and live in your home, don't you think she's good enough to marry your father? Or would you rather he marry one of those gold digging old biddies at the country club?" I asked.

Mr. Thornton started laughing. Seeing his wife's face, he placed his hand over his mouth and tried to cover it up with a fake cough. Pretty soon they were all laughing. I was just grateful not to be on the spot. I wondered if it would be okay to just sneak out while everyone was laughing, but it would be rude and I thought I'd been bordering on that since I'd gotten here.

"So, I guess if everything is okay, I'll be leaving," I said to no one in particular.

"I'll show you out," Mr. Thornton said.

"Oh, that's not necessary," I said.

"I insist."

I had known he was going to say that. Well, damn. I followed him down the same hall I'd only a few minutes before followed his wife down, but in the opposite direction. I figured it was his job to give me the bad news to not expect to get paid for my *work*. It was a good thing I could return the equipment or I'd be bouncing checks all over town. We got to the door and Mr. Thornton turned toward me.

"Miss Murphy, I can't believe my wife hired you. She must have found your business card on my desk."

"You have one of my business cards?" I asked.

"Yes, a friend of mine, Jack Benton, gave it to me. He said you helped him."

Since discretion was a huge part of my job I stood there with what I sincerely hoped was a blank look on my face.

Mr. Thornton smiled. "Good. I'm glad that he was right about you. I would like to have you help me with a little matter at my company."

"Of course. Just call me and we can set up a meeting," I said.

"That would be great. I also have a friend who is going to need some assistance." Mr. Thornton took a card out of his pocket and handed it to me.

I glanced down at the card and saw a name written on the back of it. "I'm not sure I could be of any help to your friend." I looked back up at him and attempted to hand the card to him but he refused to take it.

"Just please meet with him. If after you've talked with him you don't want any part of it, that's it. No pressure."

"Fine, but no promises," I said, sliding the card into my own pocket.

"Thank you." He opened the door and I walked out without saying another word.

Eager to escape before they changed their mind about wanting their money back, I practically ran back to my car. Once safely ensconced inside, I sighed with relief. A feeling that was short-lived. The name on the back of the card Mr. Thornton had given me was a name I recognized all too well. Nathan Larson had been front page news for months. His girlfriend, Beverly Healey, had disappeared. Searchers had found her badly beaten body in a storm drain. It was awful.

The family, especially the sister, was convinced that the boyfriend was guilty. I was pretty sure I didn't want to be involved with that case. When I got home I went to toss the card in the trash but instead I placed it on the kitchen counter next to the phone. Since I was already in the kitchen I decided it was only reasonable I search it for chocolate. It took less than thirty seconds to find the last Hershey's Bar. I stood there and ate the bar, enjoying each and every glorious bite. When it was gone, all too soon, I decided to call it a day.

Upstairs, I stripped out of my clothes, pulled a Tinker Bell nightshirt on over my head, and crawled under the covers, where I tossed and turned for hours.

CHAPTER SEVEN

The next morning when the alarm went off, I wondered how long of a prison sentence I'd get for shooting that damned thing right between the hour and the minutes. Deciding it wasn't worth it, I shut it off and dragged myself out of bed, stripped, and got into the shower. Half an hour later when I stepped out of the bathroom, I felt slightly better, but I was in desperate need of caffeine before I could face this day.

Downstairs in the kitchen, I started a pot of coffee then began the process of making the monumental decision of what to have for breakfast. Since the last thing I wanted to do was cook, my options were limited to one lonely strawberry Pop-Tart or a handful of Crunch Berries. I decided to mull it over while I drank my first cup of coffee. I had just settled on both when the doorbell rang. I took my coffee with me and looked through the peephole and smiled at the Bob Evans bag that someone was holding up. I unlocked and opened the door.

"I'm not complaining, but shouldn't you have seen who it was before you opened the door?" Zack said.

"No need to worry. If you'd turned out to be a psychopath, I'd have shot you."

"I know you meant that to be comforting, but I'd have to categorize that as terrifying."

"Whatever. You coming in or are you just going to stand there tempting me?" I asked.

"So you want me to come inside and tempt you? I'm good with that," Zack said before brushing past me.

I'd never admit it but I'd been thrilled to see him when I'd opened the door, but a part of me had been hoping to see Grant standing there. It seemed they each owned half of my heart. I just wondered who'd claim it all.

"Ass," I muttered. Zack laughed as I closed the door. He followed me into the kitchen.

"Why yes, I'd love some coffee."

I filled a mug and handed it to him. "What's in the bag?" I asked

"Scrambled eggs, bacon, home fries, biscuits, and, of course, sausage gravy."

"You're a good man. I could kiss you."

"I thought food was the way to a man's heart, not a woman's," Zack said.

"Hah. If you want my heart, you're gonna have to do better than takeout."

"I'll keep that in mind."

We took our coffee and food into the dining room. "So, what are you doing here, besides bringing me breakfast?" I asked.

"Can't I just drop by?"

"Yes, but you should be in the office by now. You show up this late and your dad would send a search party out looking for you."

"Funny. Shandra wanted me to be there this morning," Zack said.

"So then Shandra suspects it's bad."

Zack nodded.

"Oh goody."

And just like that the mood in the room went from flirty and playful to downright depressing. We finished our breakfast in silence and despite his offer of a lift, I followed Zack to Aunt Tessa's house.

We parked on the street and walked up the front walk together. He rang the doorbell and Charmaine opened the door.

"Thank goodness. I thought you two would never get here," Charmaine said.

"We're five minutes early," I pointed out.

"Whatever, just get in here."

Zack and I followed her down the hall and into the living room. Shandra, Melissa, and Aunt Tessa were already seated and waiting for us.

"Hello, everyone," Zack said.

"We can skip the greetings. Let's get this over with."

"Charmaine, I will not have you be rude to guests in my home," Aunt Tessa said.

"Yes, ma'am."

Zack and I spent the next half hour going over everything that was in the files the prosecutor had turned over. This case was on the fast track because

Lakeview, Ohio didn't get a lot of murder cases. Well, as long as you didn't count the several drug dealing kidnappers I'd killed, but those were cases of self-defense and so not the same thing. I was grateful the courts saw it that way and would be mighty pleased if the big guy upstairs agreed. I didn't think my eternal soul should be at risk for ridding the world of those losers.

Eventually they ran out of questions while Zack and I ran out of answers. We all said our goodbyes and Zack got in his car and I got in mine. With Aunt Tessa's preliminary trial set to start in three weeks, that didn't leave me much time to find the real killer.

I decided to start with Mr. Patterson's place of employment. According to the file, that would be Ohio's Premier Ace Roofing Company. I drove down First Street and pulled into the parking lot in front of the building housing the roofing company, along with a smoothie store, sub shop, and a coffee shop.

Personally, I thought that an odd location for a roofing company, but then again, what the hell did I know. I walked inside and was surprised to see how empty and temporary the place looked. There was a long metal table surrounded by folding chairs. On top of the table were flyers with the company name on it. On the floor against the wall were company signs to stick in people's front yards.

I was the only one in the room. If this hadn't been so important, I would have left and gone next door to get a banana kiwi smoothie. I'd wait another minute or two and if no one came out to help me,

I'd start poking my head in doors until I found someone or something of interest. I walked over to the table and picked up a flyer. I was sliding it into my purse when I heard a woman's voice.

"Can I help you with something?"

I turned around and found a woman in her forties with black hair, dark eyes, and wearing way too much makeup standing in the hall.

My instinct was to lie but I decided to go with the truth this time. "Hello, I'm here to speak with a manager or an owner."

"I'm Tanya Tipton, co-owner. How can I help you?" she asked.

I introduced myself and sort of explained why I was there. Since she knew the victim, I didn't think it wise for her to know I was working for the defense. She didn't seem offended and invited me into her office. I sat down across from her desk in a metal folding chair. I assumed the office of a co-owner of a roofing company would have better office furniture than me but actually the stuff I'd lost in the fire was better than this stuff. Plus, there was no heavy cigarette smell in mine, although now I was dealing with new carpet and paint fumes.

"So, what can I do for you?" she asked before lighting up a cigarette and inhaling.

I stared with a longing I thought was gone. Seeing my desperation, she picked up the pack and offered me one. I shook my head as if to clear my brain and declined. Not from any willpower but because I had been a dedicated menthol smoker while she was not.

"Ms. Tipton, according to my files, Mr.

Patterson was the owner of this company."

"That's Mrs. Tipton," she said, waving her left hand at me with a rock big enough to need its own security team. "Derek co-owns, I mean, co-owned the company with me and my husband," she said.

"Oh. How long have you been in business?" I asked.

"Five years."

"Wow. That's great. Have you always been in this location?"

"No, we just relocated a few months ago. Derek was from this part of Ohio and for some strange reason he wanted to come home."

"Where were you located before?"

Mrs. Tipton fidgeted with her ring. "Cleveland."

"Anywhere else?" I asked.

"Look, I don't know what any of this has to do with Derek's killer. He was a wonderful man. I just don't understand why anyone would kill him," she said, grabbing a tissue and wiping the tears from her eyes.

"I'm just trying to get some basic information. Was he having trouble with anyone? Problems at home or with a client?" I asked.

"Of course not. Everyone loved Derek. Although he and Shaina were going through a rough patch, but I'm sure she had nothing to do with it."

"What kind of rough patch?"

"She was desperate to have kids. I don't understand why. I never felt the urge to have some smelly, disgusting kids hanging off of me."

Though I wasn't in any rush to be someone's mother, I didn't think of my numerous nieces and nephews as smelly, disgusting creatures. It was probably a good thing she hadn't procreated.

"So, what was the problem? Infertility?" I asked.

"No way. Derek was virile. No, he didn't want to have kids. That stupid witch. He told her that before they got married but the second he gave in and married her she tried to talk him into it."

"If she was that desperate, I'm surprised she didn't *accidently* get pregnant," I said.

"Oh, there would have been none of that. Shaina may have stopped taking her birth control pills but Derek wasn't stupid. He insisted on wearing a condom. Always."

I had no idea what to say after that. I got that they were business partners, but that seemed like rather intimate details to have shared with someone. I could see having that discussion with my best friends, but even then that would be kind of a bit uncomfortable.

"So, you're sure he didn't have any enemies? Maybe a competitor? An unhappy client?"

"Of course not. Our company has an A plus rating with the Better Business Bureau."

"That's great, but surely you've had at least one disgruntled former employee or an unsatisfied client. Could I speak to your husband?"

"I think it's time for you to leave." Mrs. Tipton stood up and so did I. She followed me to the front door. I reached into my purse and tried to hand her my business card. Mrs. Tipton looked down at it and frowned. "No thanks." She opened the door and I stepped through. I started to thank her for her time but she shut and locked the door.

"Well, that was fun." I got into my car and considered who I should question or harass next. I hated it but really I had little choice but to head straight for the grieving widow. Who knew, maybe she wasn't grieving so much if what Mrs. Tipton said was accurate.

I checked the address and turned on the car. The blast of hot air to the face was unsettling and unwelcomed but luckily it would soon be replaced with arctic cold air. The weatherman had promised rain later this afternoon followed by a cool front. I would be grateful for the temporary relief. As much as I enjoyed summer, I preferred fall weather in Ohio as it was usually not too hot and not too cold, just like the porridge that Goldilocks settled on. There was also the added bonus of the leaves changing color and pumpkin-flavored goodies from cookies and pies to coffees and creamers.

I put the car in gear and headed south to Oakdale. By the time I arrived at the address the car had cooled off and I was loath to leave it. I parked in front of a large Tudor-style home and considered my approach.

I got out of my car and walked up the front walkway to the door. I rang the doorbell and waited. Eventually a blonde woman my age in a red silk robe with bags under her unnaturally blue eyes and her hair in curlers opened the door.

"Yeah."

"Hello, I'm sorry to disturb you. I'm looking for Mrs. Patterson," I said

"Lucky you. You found her. Unless you mean that bitch of a mother-in-law of mine, in which case you'll have to check with the Devil to see if she's available."

I smiled. I had wished that fate a time or two on my former in-laws. "My name is Kim Murphy. I'm sorry to bother you, but I'm investigating your husband's death."

"Well, it's about damned time." She stepped aside and ushered me inside. "I've been calling and calling, and those damned detectives of yours haven't bothered to return a single call."

So once again, through no fault of my own, I was being mistaken for a police officer. Now there were two ways I could handle it. I could be truthful and get shown the door or just go along with it, making sure not to say I was a cop, and see what she'd tell me. Since the first option would most likely get me booted, I chose to go with the second one.

I followed her through the house overstuffed with furniture and into the kitchen which suffered the same fate of way too many things in the space. I thought it an odd place to talk until I saw the half-empty bottle of wine and a half-filled wine glass on the kitchen island. She sat down and with one hand gestured for me to have a seat while grabbing the glass with her other hand.

"So, what can you tell me? And don't give me anymore crap about it being an ongoing investigation."

"Well, Mrs. Patterson, as you know, a suspect has been arrested in your husband's murder."

"Yeah, I still don't understand that. Why would some little old lady I've never even heard of kill my Derek? It doesn't make sense."

I didn't think it did either but I thought it best to keep that thought to myself. "So, I'm going over everything. Would it be all right if I asked you some questions?"

"Lady, you can ask me anything you want."

"Okay, great." I took out a small notebook and pretended to be reading over my notes. "So, when did you report your husband missing?"

"The day before his body was found."

"Hadn't he been missing for two days at that point?" I asked.

"I guess, but I was out of town and I didn't realize he hadn't been home."

"When was the last time you spoke with your husband?"

"The day before he died. We talked on the phone that morning and then I'd texted him that evening but he never texted me back."

"Was that unusual?"

"Yes. I was worried but I just thought he was tired and had gone to bed early. I got home the next day and when he hadn't returned my phone calls or texts I knew something was wrong."

"Was anything out of place in your house or anything missing?" I asked.

"No. I don't think so."

"Did your husband have any enemies? How about any problems with neighbors or family members?"

"No. Derek was a good man. All that's left of his family is his drunk of a mother and his brother."

"Did they have any arguments lately?"

"No more than usual. His mother did come

around asking for money again."

"Did your husband give it to her?" I asked.

"Of course. He could never say no to that woman."

"Did the two of you disagree about his helping her?"

Mrs. Patterson set her glass down and looked me in the eye. "Yes. I argued with him every time he helped her but she was his mom. There was no way I was going to win that battle."

"Did the two of you have any other disagreements?"

"Of course we argued. We were married. That doesn't mean I killed him."

I looked back up from my notebook.

"Don't look so surprised. I could tell where that was headed. That hot detective they sent out was grilling me about where I was and what I was doing. I was so glad I had an alibi or the idiot would have carted me off to jail."

"Where were you when your husband disappeared?" I asked, choosing to ignore the whole hot detective thing. Okay, I was trying to ignore the comment, but I really just wanted to knock her teeth out.

"I was at my sister's. She had just broken up with her boyfriend, again, and was miserable. I went and stayed the night." Mrs. Patterson reached into her purse and pulled out a pack of cigarettes. When she turned to reach for a lighter, her purse fell, spilling the contents onto the floor. "Shit." She looked as if she was about to burst into tears.

"I'll get it." I reached down and stuffed a pair of

sunglasses, a pack of gum, a pack of birth control pills, and hairbrush into her Coach bag.

"Thanks."

I placed the purse on the counter and sat back down. "If you had really wanted your husband dead, you could have hired someone to do it and made sure you had an airtight alibi," I said.

"True, but I loved him. I sure as heck didn't want him dead. He pissed me off sometimes but that's what husbands do."

And here I'd thought it had just been my ex-husband who'd had the annoying gift of pissing people off. "No major issues?" I asked.

"No."

"It says that you had wanted to start a family but that your husband refused."

Mrs. Patterson slammed her glass down on the granite counter top. "That bitch. I know exactly who told you that. My husband's latest fling."

"Mrs. Tipton?" I asked.

"Yup. Can you believe it? He had me here at home, willing to do anything for him, but he'd gone and screwed Tanya. What he saw in that old hag, I'll never know."

"Weren't you angry about the affair?"

Mrs. Patterson poured more wine into her glass before picking it up. "Nope. I figured if he could play, so could I."

"So, you were also having an affair?"

"I wouldn't call them affairs, more like wild sexual escapades with a side benefit of getting even."

"Did Mr. Patterson know about these

escapades?"

"Of course. That was the whole point. My whole trip to the spa had been a nice few days away with someone I knew would send him running right home to me where he belongs…belonged."

"Why would this person have mattered?"

"It was his business partner, Carl."

"Tipton? Like, as in Tanya Tipton's husband?" I asked.

"Yup. I can't wait to see that bitch's face when she finds out while she was screwing my husband, I was screwing hers." She smiled before taking a huge sip from her glass.

I sat for a moment processing that while she continued to drink. It took a minute or so before I was able to ask any more questions. "So, were the two of you having any financial difficulties?"

"No. We're good." She looked around the room. "I guess it's just me now, and thanks to his business and life insurance, I'm set for life."

"What about his family?"

"According to the will, they get nothing. He said he was done supporting them."

Unsure of what to say, I just nodded.

"You know, I'd give it all to them to have him back," Mrs. Patterson said before bursting into tears.

Awkward around strangers' emotions, I rushed up and grabbed a handful of napkins and stuffed them into her hands. I mumbled some encouraging words; at least I hoped they were. I was extremely relieved when she seemed better. I gave her my condolences and assured her I would let her know if

I discovered anything else.

I was so eager to escape that even the cloying heat in the car was a welcome relief. While the car air conditioner tried to bring the sauna level heat down to bearable, I jotted down notes about what I'd learned. Granted, it wasn't much, but it was something. I now had several more people to talk to: the victim's mother and brother, plus his business partner—the one he wasn't sleeping with.

I did a little search and found that Mr. Patterson's mother lived just south of downtown Lakeview. I put down the notes, put the car in gear, and headed back across town. Twenty minutes later, I parked in front of Mrs. Patterson's apartment complex.

The one-story building held four apartments. On the other side of the walkway was an identical replica of white brick, red shutters, and red front doors. I waited a moment to see if I would talk myself out of this, but when that didn't happen, I got out of my car and walked up to the building. I knocked on the door and waited.

A blonde woman in a pink blouse and black slacks opened the door. "Yeah."

"Hello, I'm looking for a Mrs. Patterson," I said.

"Good for you. You found me," she said.

"Oh, okay. My name is Kim Murphy. I'm sorry to bother you, but I'm investigating your son's murder," I said

"Murder? I thought he fell off a roof," she said.

"What?"

"I could have sworn that's what that slut daughter-in-law of mine said."

"Haven't you spoken with the police department?" I asked.

"Maybe, I don't know. Some young fella came around here askin' me questions. I told him to get lost. I don't like cops."

"They can be a real pain," I said, silently apologizing to all the cops in my family and even a certain cop who wasn't too fond of me right now.

"Yeah. So, what do you care what happened to my kid?" She swayed a little from side to side. She grabbed onto the doorframe and held on with both hands.

"Just doing my job," I said.

"Is there gonna be some kind of lawsuit or somethin', because I sure could use the money."

The last thing Aunt Tessa needed was a lawsuit from these people. "I'm not sure. You'd have to ask his wife," I said.

"Agh, that greedy slut. She made sure I was left out of his will. She'll make damned sure I wouldn't get a dime in a lawsuit. Too bad she didn't fall off of a house."

Wow, and I thought my family had issues. This one was a mess. Since I didn't think I'd be getting anything helpful from her, I thanked her for her time and turned to leave.

"Maybe I could sue that no good daughter-in-law of mine."

"Huh, that's a thought," I said, and headed back to my car. I figured since today had been a total bust I should try talking to the victim's brother to round out the day before giving up and going home. Once again I dug out the notebook from my purse and with a little Internet search I found Mr. Evan Patterson.

I decided to go ahead and drive the twenty-five minutes to downtown Dayton and try to talk to the victim's brother. To avoid road rage during the beginning of rush hour traffic, I stuck Maroon 5's latest CD in the player and cranked up the volume. Adam Levine could almost always put a smile on my face, and he didn't even have to sing. He could just stand there and look hot. In my fantasy his whole marrying a model thing never happened.

I avoided downtown as much as possible. Not because I didn't like it but because I loathed parallel parking and having to pay for the privilege of such a torture. Plus, there were all those damned one-way streets that always seemed to go the opposite way I needed to travel.

I found an empty spot half a block away from Mr. Patterson's apartment building. I zipped in and scrounged in my purse for change. I found what I hoped would be enough. I looked up and jerked back, sending my change scattering.

"Lady, can you stop screaming?" the parking meter lady said.

I closed my mouth and rolled my window down several inches. "Yes?"

"Your meter's expired," she said, pointing to the meter as if I didn't know where it was located.

"Yeah, well, I just pulled into the spot. The car's still running. I was looking for change and I haven't gotten out of the car yet," I said.

She sighed. "Fine. I'll give you a warning this time, but don't let it happen again." She turned and walked back to her car.

I rolled up the window and muttered, "Gee, thanks." I couldn't believe she was acting like she'd done me a huge favor.

I looked over and she waved at me. I plastered a fake smile on my face and waved back. Only I would get the crazy parking meter lady. I turned off the car, scooped up all the change, and got out of my car, rushing over to feed the meter in case she came back or one of her buddies came along and gave me a ticket.

I had just enough change to park in the spot for forty-five minutes. I could use my credit card but there was no way in hell I would do that. That meant I'd have to walk and talk fast. I speed walked and stopped in front of an ugly brown five-story building.

Since the only kind of luck I had was crappy, Mr. Patterson, the still alive brother, lived on the fifth floor. I checked by the front door to see if I needed to be buzzed in or not but this building didn't seem to have any security measures at all.

One look at the creaky, dark elevators had me imagining plunging to my death. The authorities would find my body being feasted on by rats. I turned and headed straight for the stairs. I was all set to grumble to myself about having to walk up five sets of stairs until I realized I'd skipped the gym yet again. This would be the perfect cardio activity and it was free. I hated every freaking second of it but at least I was in good enough shape I only felt slightly out of breath, and I barely felt dizzy at all.

I walked to the end of the hall and knocked on the door. A man in his twenties, who looked startlingly like the dead guy, opened the door. "Whatever you're sellin', I'm buyin'," he said.

Yuck. He was dressed in navy dress pants, a dark blue suit jacket, and a blue and white striped tie. I looked at him and tried my best to smile. "Hello, Mr. Patterson, I'm investigating your brother's murder. Do you have a few minutes so we could talk?"

"For you? Sure thing. Come on in." He stepped aside and I felt an urge to run away, far away. Since that wouldn't be professional, I smiled and walked inside. His apartment was less bachelor pad more grandma style with a flower patterned couch and wallpaper. The carpet was old and dingy while the place smelled of cigarette smoke and cooked cabbage.

"Here, have a seat." He walked over and slid a stack of papers off the couch so there would be room for me to sit.

"Thanks." I sat on the very edge of the seat.

"So, what can I do for you?" he asked as he sat down in a reclining chair across from me.

"Well, as I said, I'm looking into your brother's murder. Did you know if your brother was having problems with anyone?" I asked.

He laughed and pointed to the small notebook I held in my hand. "You're going to need more paper than that," he said.

Surprised, I felt my eyebrows rise in disbelief at the blunt honesty. "Wow. That bad, huh?"

"Oh yeah. Derek was a real charmer. He was

also a liar and a cheater."

"Anyone specific making threats?"

"He got lots of threats but I don't think any of them were serious."

"What about friends or family members? Did any of them have a problem with Derek?"

"Just about everybody had problems with my brother. I just can't believe any of them were mad enough to have killed him."

He tilted his head and rubbed his chin. I didn't want to interrupt his thought process so I sat quietly and waited. It wasn't long before I was rewarded, sort of, for my patience.

"I know he had a few customers who were threatening to sue him. Plus, there was his affair with his business partner's wife. I'm pretty sure if Carl had found out, he'd have killed Derek."

"So, Mr. Tipton has a temper?" I asked.

"He sure does. Just last month, Carl and Derek about came to blows. I had to step in," he said.

"What were they arguing about?"

"Something about the business. Later, I asked Derek but he said it was no big deal."

"I would think it a pretty big deal if it was about to get physical," I said.

Mr. Patterson laughed. "That's what I thought too."

This was good news for Aunt Tessa. I had to keep reminding myself not to smile. "Can you think of anyone else who might have wanted to harm your brother?"

"His wife, my mother, plus the clients he ripped off. My brother was not a good man. Hell, even I'd taken a swing at him a few times."

"Oh really?"

"Don't look at me like that." He folded his arms across his chest. "I didn't kill him. It was just sibling stuff. You have a brother?" he asked.

"Four of them, plus a sister. They're only extremely annoying."

He laughed. "Then you know how it is."

"Yeah, but I wouldn't mind hearing about your alibi for the time of your brother's murder," I said.

Mr. Patterson grimaced.

"Sorry."

"No problem. I was working."

"Can anyone vouch for you?" I asked.

"Yeah. I work at the Lakeview Organic Market."

"That place is expensive."

"Oh yeah. You want eighteen quail eggs? That'll set you back ten dollars," he said.

"Quail eggs?"

"Yeah, they're smaller than robin eggs. So, if you want an omelet, you'll have to use two containers. How's twenty dollars for an omelet sound?" he asked

"Insane."

"True, but I have one customer who swears they're the best eggs she's ever had."

"Maybe, but I'll pass." Figuring I had probably gotten everything useful I could out of Mr. Patterson, I stood up and thanked him for his time. He followed me to the front door and reached around me for the doorknob. I handed him one of my business cards and asked him to call me if he thought of anything else. I stepped into the hallway.

"I'm sorry for your loss."

"Thanks. I just wish I felt bad about his death," he said.

He closed the door and I thought about how sad that was. With all four of my brothers being cops, two of them as members of SWAT, there was a chance that one of them could pay the ultimate price to keep our city safe. I shuddered at the thought. The death of one or more of them would be unimaginable. I prayed my family never had to suffer such a loss.

A glance at my watch had me racing down all five flights of stairs, out the door, and up the block to my car. I was half expecting to see the *friendly* parking meter woman standing next to my car waving a ticket around.

Back in my car, I pulled my cell phone from my purse. I had missed a call from Shandra. I wasn't eager to return her call, which was exactly what she asked me to do on her message. So far I hadn't learned anything that could clear Aunt Tessa's name. I dialed the number and waited silently, hoping to get voice mail.

"Kim, thank goodness you got my message."

"I did. What's up?"

"Aunt Tessa wants you to join us for dinner."

"Oh, I don't know, I've kind of got stuff to do," I lied.

"Well, unless you have a hot date, Aunt Tessa won't be taking no for an answer."

"Fine. I'll see you around six." Dinner at Aunt Tessa's was always served at six, never a minute before or after.

"Good. See you later."

I hung up and watched as the flashing light on the parking meter changed from green to red. It was time to get out of downtown. I started the car and headed for Lakeview. Halfway home my landlord called to inform me my office remodel was finished, a full three days ahead of schedule. I decided to take the detour and see it for myself.

I parked in the back lot and let myself in with my set of new keys. A brand new alarm system had also been installed. It took me a couple of seconds before I remembered the code. I punched it in and was relieved when I shut the alarm off instead of setting it off as I had done previously.

I flipped lights on as I went into each room. Other than the color choice, I was pleased with how it had turned out. In the closet-size kitchen, I noticed that for some strange reason my landlord had given me a new coffeemaker, the kind you put those little pre-measured cups in. That was odd since the fire hadn't spread that far, but as a coffee addict I was extremely grateful for the new device that promised to provide me with my daily shots of much needed caffeine.

In my office, all of the new furniture, my desk, chairs, and a filing cabinet, had been arranged just like I'd had the room previously set up. Now, though, there were framed paintings on the wall. It felt like I was in a doctor's office, minus the stacks of paper and medical college degrees on the walls. The place was so neat and tidy I wondered how long it would take me to have it cluttered up again. Sigh.

I sat down at my new desk. I breathed in the smell of new carpet, paint, and furniture. I began to cough. I'd have to come back in the next day or two and let the place air out. It wouldn't be good for business if prospective clients began passing out on me.

I rearranged the placement of my new phone, tape dispenser, and stapler. My new laptop was shiny and tempting in the center of the desk. I opened the desk drawers and found them empty. I would need to make a run to the store for office supplies. I mean, whoever heard of an office without staples, paperclips, and an emergency supply of snacks, preferably of the chocolate variety?

With some regret I got up from my new and much comfier chair and began to turn off all the lights I had turned on. I reset the alarm, stepped outside the door, and locked it. I turned around and barely stifled a scream. Standing a few feet away from me were two men, each well over six feet tall, both in black suits and ties, and with the same short haircuts.

"Miss Murphy, we need you to come with us," the one on the left said.

"Well, as tempting as that sounds, I'll have to pass," I replied.

"No is not an option," the one on the right said.

I looked from one to the other. "You don't want to do this," I said.

The two of them moved toward me. Any second I'd be pinned against the building. That didn't mean I'd be helpless, even if I couldn't reach my gun.

They moved closer and each reached out for my arms. I spun around and elbowed one in the face while kicking the other in the knee. Sadly, the struggle was over shortly and I was stuffed into the back of a black limousine, nestled between the two extremely muscular behemoths.

Twenty minutes later the limo pulled up in front of a house large enough to hide several airplanes, a helicopter, and a small grocery store with room leftover for a hair salon. I was escorted up the front steps and into a two-story foyer. I found myself staring at double staircases on either side. Our little threesome walked down a long hall with vividly colored paintings on the wall. At the end of the hall a brown wood paneled door opened and I was escorted inside.

It was completely inappropriate but I found myself staring at the extremely handsome man sitting behind a desk big enough to host a dinner party for ten.

"Miss Murphy, I'm so glad you could come," Mr. Nathan Larson said.

He stood up and stuck out his hand. When I didn't take it, one of his Neanderthals nudged me forward. I shook it and released it almost immediately. It was odd but somehow he was even better-looking in person than on HD TV. His blue eyes sparkled and his smile revealed laugh lines. Not a single blond hair was out of place.

"Yes, well, it seems I didn't have much of a choice." I tilted my head side to side indicating his goons.

"Sorry about that. My employees tend to be a bit

determined." He looked at them and dismissed them.

"You might want to put a steak on that shiner. I hear it helps," I said to the one I'd hit in the face with my elbow. His companion chuckled. "Yeah, and you might need to put some ice on that leg." I laughed when he frowned at me before limping off.

"Please, have a seat," Mr. Larson said, pointing at the two chairs across from him. I considered refusing but decided it was too juvenile.

"Thanks." I sat down. "You know, as far as kidnappings go, this is by far the classiest one I've ever had. I mean, a limo? Nice."

Mr. Larson laughed. "I like you."

I wasn't sure if that was a good thing or a bad thing. I assumed he had liked his girlfriend but he was the prime suspect in her murder. So I smiled as not to offend him. A smile I hoped was not too fake or too encouraging.

"I assume you are aware of my situation."

"Yes," I said, though I'd never thought of being charged with murder as a *situation* before.

"Well, I want to hire you. According to my sources, you are the best."

"You want to hire me to do what?" I asked.

"Why, find the real killer, of course," he said.

Oh hell. This was not good. Unfortunately, no one in my family had been responsible for Mr. Larson's arrest, so I couldn't use that conflict of interest as an excuse. Even Grant hadn't been involved with this case. Damn.

"I'm sorry, Mr. Larson, as much as I'd love to help, I'm just swamped with too many clients right now," I lied. "I'd be more than happy to give you a few names of excellent agencies that could help you."

"I'm sure you could, but I want you."

I swallowed but it sounded like a gulp in my ears. "That's nice of you, but really, I wouldn't be able to give your case the type of attention it needs."

"I understand."

"Okay, then." I stood up relieved and eager to leave.

"I also understand you're a businesswoman. I'm innocent. I'll pay you twenty thousand dollars. Find the real killer and I'll add another ten thousand on top of that."

I felt my lower jaw drop open. "Mr. Larson, it really isn't about the money," I said after I could get my mouth to work. "Why do you want me?"

"Miss Murphy, I want the best, and according to my head of security, you're it."

"While that's flattering, I think it's a stretch. We're talking about your freedom. Wouldn't you feel more comfortable using a large investigative firm?"

"Now you sound like my lawyer." He laughed. "Nope. Over the years I've learned to trust my instinct, and right now it is telling me we'll be a good match."

I sincerely hoped he meant in an employee to employer kind of way and not in a personal way. I had enough trouble with two men in my life. The last thing I needed was a rich stalker who just might have killed his previous match.

125

I stood there desperately thinking of a way to decline his generous offer. He must have sensed my reluctance because he stood and placed his hand on mine. The contact gave my pulse a jump start. The words *murder suspect* kept floating around in my mind. I gently slid my hand away from his.

He sighed. "Lots of people claim they're innocent. Some are and some aren't. I give you my word. I could have never hurt, much less killed, Beverly." He ran his hands through his hair, causing a tussled look. "I'll make you a deal. I will give you unfettered access to my life. No questions off limits. You find anything that says I'm guilty and I'll confess."

I stared at him, looking for any outward sign that he suffered from some form of mental illness. All I saw was a handsome, desperate man in a suit, no tie, and willing to pay me a boatload of money.

"You know, I have an aunt who would say you were batshit crazy."

He laughed. "And what do you think?"

"I'm thinking maybe it could be contagious."

"Excellent."

"Look, right now I'm working on a case that's very important to me. That comes first."

"I understand."

"Good. Also, if I agree to take your case, I'll charge you the same amount I charge all my other clients."

"That's more than fair. Would you care to stay for dinner?"

"Sorry, I've got work to do."

"Another time, then." He reached into his pocket

and pulled out a card. "Here's my card. I've written my cell number on the back," he said, handing it to me.

I didn't think he realized how that sounded. If the jury convicted him, he'd have a whole other kind of cell number. Since I didn't think he'd appreciate me pointing that out to him, I kept my mouth shut on the matter. I took the card and stuffed it into my purse. "Thanks."

"I'll have Dominic take you home," Mr. Larson said.

"As long as Dominic is the driver. I'm pretty sure I don't need Frick and Frack escorting me," I said as I headed for the door.

"Of course." He sat back down at his desk and picked up a cell phone. "I look forward to seeing you tomorrow."

I didn't know what to say so I just nodded and rushed out of the room. The drive back was more pleasant without the giant bookends but it felt weird to be in the back of a limousine all by myself. I practically jumped out of the car before it came to a complete stop at my office.

I got in my car and headed home. Inside my apartment, I rushed upstairs and into the bathroom. I had just enough time to shower and get dressed for dinner. I even spent time drying my hair and applying makeup. I tossed the standard little black dress over my head and shoved my size eights into a pair of wedge heeled sandals.

I blasted the radio to keep my mind from focusing on just why I'd taken Mr. Larson's case. It would do no good to dig too deeply into it, though soon enough I would be delving quite thoroughly into his life. If he thought because I was a woman I'd go easy on him, he would soon learn his mistake. I was like a cougar stalking her prey. I didn't give up because there was too much at stake. Or was that steak?

I parked my car in front of Aunt Tessa's house. I was more than a little surprised when Zack's Porsche pulled up and parked behind my car. "What are you doing here?" I asked.

"I was invited. You know I can't pass up a free home-cooked meal."

I couldn't argue with his reasoning. The free food had been a huge part of the reason I'd agreed to attend tonight. "Fine. You can stay but you'd better behave."

Zack pulled me up against him. "Are you sure you want me to behave?" he whispered in my ear, sending tingling sensations racing all over my body and settling into some private parts that were suddenly all too eager for the close contact. I desperately wanted to drag him into my roomier car. My hands ached to rip off his clothes and touch every glorious part of him. I heard a small groan and realized I was the one making the sound. I opened my eyes with no memory of having closed them.

The sun hadn't set yet and I realized the two of us were standing on the sidewalk rubbing against each other like a couple of teenagers in heat. It took every ounce of willpower I had, but I broke free and stepped back. "We can't do this," I said, surprised by how shaky my voice was.

"You're right." He stuffed his hands into his pockets. "I hate it, but you're right."

"Okay," I said, but I didn't feel okay. I felt frustrated and confused.

We walked side by side up to the front door. Zack rang the bell and we stood there silently waiting. Dressed in a yellow blouse and beige slacks, Shandra opened the door and smiled when she saw us. "Come in. I'm so glad you're here. Charmaine is driving me crazy."

I laughed. "Good, then everything is back to normal." Shandra gave me a hug and then reached over and planted a kiss on Zack's cheek, just like she'd done hundreds of other times. Only this time I felt a twinge of jealousy. This was insane. I had to get a grip. I shook my head in an attempt to clear out the cobwebs then headed down the hall with Shandra and Zack following behind me.

I walked into the kitchen and saw Aunt Tessa, her gray hair pulled back with a silver barrette, standing over the sink with a pan in her hand. She turned and saw me, her face lit up with her smile. Aunt Tessa set the pan on the stove then walked over and threw her arms around me. I was instantly surrounded by the scent of Calvin Klein's Obsession and the delicious smells of food cooking. Aunt Tessa let go of me, stepped back, then promptly announced I was too pale, too skinny, and had bags under my eyes. I smiled because she always told me these things.

"I promise to get more sleep and to clean my plate. I tried to do something about the pale Irish complexion my dad passed on, but all I managed to do was get a sunburn."

"You should have known better. No more sun for you."

"I know."

"Good. Now go sit." She turned and Zack stepped into her open arms. He was also told he needed to get more rest and should eat more.

I laughed. I'd seen Zack down an entire sausage and mushroom pizza on numerous occasions. The man ate plenty. He just was a regular at his gym. I'd say those daily visits did wonders for removing any and all traces of the fast food he lived on. As I had seen and touched every delicious inch of him, I said a silent prayer of thanks to the man upstairs.

Charmaine walked over and practically dragged me from the kitchen. "Thank God you're here. What have you found out?" she asked.

"Well, I—"

"Charmaine, quit pesterin' her. It is time for supper. Now sit down and you can say grace."

"Yes, ma'am."

We each took our seats and yet again Zack had somehow managed to sit next to me. I scowled at him but all he did was smile in return. It was understood there would be no discussion about the case while we ate so the conversation revolved around small talk like sports and the weather. After a nice dinner of honey glazed ham, salad, steamed vegetables, scalloped potatoes, and dinner rolls, Aunt Tessa ushered us into the family room, having refused our offers to help clear the table.

I chose a maroon paisley accent chair. Zack would have a hard time sitting next to me now. He walked past me, his legs brushing against mine. He sat on the couch, on the opposite side of the coffee table from me. After Charmaine, Shandra, and Aunt Tessa took their seats, Zack and I took turns updating them on what we had each been working on.

"So, the dead guy was scum and lots of people hated him? That's great," Charmaine said.

"Young lady, that is a terrible thing to say about someone who has died," Aunt Tessa said.

"It is, but she's right," Shandra said from her seat on the ottoman. In unison we all turned and looked at her. "What?" she asked.

"I don't know about anybody else but I'm just a bit in shock to hear you agree with me," Charmaine replied.

"It has happened before. Not very often, but it has happened."

"Yeah, the last time was when we were kids and we could only buy one flavor of ice cream at the store. You talked me into the Neapolitan because it had three flavors in one," Charmaine said.

"That was just common sense," Shandra said.

"Would you two stop bickering and let Kim finish?"

"Yes, ma'am," Shandra and Charmaine said in unison.

"Tomorrow I'm going to try to talk to his business partner and some of his neighbors. I can stop by tomorrow night and fill you in," I said, looking at Aunt Tessa.

"Kim, you just do whatever you need to do. Don't worry about giving me daily updates because really I just want this horrible business to be over with."

"But…" Charmaine said.

Aunt Tessa lifted her hands up, palms facing us. "Nope. I've made up my mind." She turned toward me. "Kim, when you find out anything helpful, you just let Zack know and the two of you can handle this. Please."

"Of course," I said, ignoring the sudden unease in my stomach.

"Good. Now, I'm a bit tired, so if all of you young folks will excuse me."

We all stood up. Aunt Tessa gave each of us a hug and wished us goodnight. Once she was out of the room Charmaine expressed her concerns about her aunt's health like only she could. "Damn it. I hate seein' her like this. All the spunk is just gone."

"She'll get it back. Once Kim finds the real killer," Shandra said.

"Absolutely. I think it's time we called it a night," Zack said.

We said our goodbyes and once again I was alone with Zack, standing next to our cars. "So, do you think the partner will get you anywhere?" he asked me.

"I don't know. I hope so."

"Hey…" He tucked a strand of hair behind my ear. "You're doing great."

"No, I'm not."

"Kim, you've already established there are other people who wanted the victim dead. That's a long way toward reasonable doubt," Zack said.

"I guess, but I'd rather find the real killer and

end this nightmare for them." I tilted my head toward the house.

"I know. You hate feeling helpless, especially when someone you care about is involved."

"It sucks." I blew out a breath.

Zack stepped over and wrapped his arms around me. I froze in place. "Relax. I know you'll do whatever it takes. I have faith in you."

I said nothing. I couldn't. There were tears that threatened to stream down my face. We just stood there for a moment. Just as I thought I could speak, Zack's phone rang. I stepped back. He reached for his phone and sighed at the display. He stuffed it back into his pocket.

"You better deal with that."

"Eve Sumner can wait," he said.

"Who's Eve?" I asked. "Wait. Sorry, that's none of my business."

"You've already met her. At your mom's birthday party."

"Oh right. The slutty blonde. Sorry, I forgot. Getting kidnapped and almost murdered tends to mess with the memory a little."

"I don't know about the slutty part."

"Shouldn't you call her back?" I asked.

"No. Whatever it is, she can tell me at dinner tomorrow night."

"Dinner? That's great. I have to go." I spun around and reached for the car door handle.

"Wait."

Zack slid his arms around me, pinning me between him and the car behind me. Under other circumstances I would appreciate our positioning, but not now. I couldn't believe he had a date with the rich bitch. I knew his dad had been encouraging the relationship; she was, after all, the ideal future daughter-in-law; rich, beautiful, and well-connected with the country club set. She was my complete opposite, the anti-me. I hated her. "Zack, let me go."

"If I didn't know better, I'd swear you were jealous," he said, ignoring my request.

"Hah. You wish."

"Oh, I think you are." Zack slid his right hand up from my waist to cup my breast. "Come back to my place," he whispered in my ear, sending chills up and down my spine. "God, I want you." He gently squeezed my breast and rubbed against my backside.

"Zack…"

"I love it when you moan. Come home with me and I promise to make you moan all night."

I was just about to give in when his cell phone rang again. "You should see who that is, it might be important," I said.

"It can wait."

"I'm sure your clients would be thrilled to hear you say that."

"Shit." He dug his phone out of his pocket.

I turned my head and looked at the screen—Eve Sumner.

"I guess she couldn't wait."

He sighed and stuck the phone back into his pocket.

"Come home with me."

"I can't. I've got work for a client," I lied.

"Okay, how about I come over after dinner tomorrow. I'll show you that you have nothing to worry about."

"Wow. How generous. Sloppy seconds, I'll pass."

"Kim…"

I opened my car door and slid into the driver's seat. Zack grabbed the door before I could close it.

"Let go."

"Not until you tell me what's going on."

I couldn't tell him that the thought of him being within a mile of the woman drove me insane. To be honest, the thought of him with any other woman made me sick to my stomach. Telling him would be selfish. Yeah, he'd dump the blonde bimbo, but eventually he'd realize I wasn't right for him, and I couldn't stand that. A little hurt now was better than that utter devastation. At least I sincerely hoped so.

"Look, we have a lot of fun but that's all there is and I think we're both getting too old for that," I said.

Zack's hands fisted at his sides. His face flushed. "Fun? Is that all we are?" he asked.

I wanted to tell him it was a lie but I couldn't. I wanted to prove to him that I loved him but that would be selfish, and I loved him enough to put his needs ahead of my own. "Exactly. I'm glad you understand." I patted his hand and pretended not to see the hurt in his eyes.

"Whatever." Zack turned away and stomped off to his car.

I drove toward home but made a detour at the grocery store. I told myself it was because I needed orange juice but I began filling the cart with ice cream—chocolate and vanilla—hot fudge, whipped topping, bananas, and mini chocolate chips. Before heading to the register I added a bottle of wine and a *People* magazine. I paid for my purchases without incident and drove home.

Back inside my apartment, I filled a large bowl with everything but the alcohol and the magazine. I took my pity party in a bowl into the living room. I plopped down on the couch and scooped up the remote and began channel surfing until I settled on *Property Brothers*. I figured if I was going to drown my sorrows in a million calories of sugary goodness, I might as well enjoy some eye candy.

Eventually the ice cream disappeared and I dragged myself upstairs. In the bathroom, I stripped out of my clothes, brushed my teeth, and washed my face. In my bedroom, I pulled a *Star Wars* nightshirt on over my head then crawled under the covers. I tossed and turned until I was finally comfortable then promptly burst into tears.

CHAPTER EIGHT

I grabbed the alarm clock and tossed it at the wall. Eventually, I had cried myself to sleep last night. My head ached as if I'd had a few too many alcoholic beverages. When I opened my eyes, my vision was blurry and all I wanted to do was hide under the covers—forever.

Since I had bills to pay and friends to help that was not an option. I crawled out of bed and picked up the still beeping alarm and shut it off. I walked into the bathroom and made the horrendous mistake of looking in the mirror. I looked like a display the Halloween stores used to frighten off small children.

I washed my face, pulled my hair up into a ponytail, and put on a pair of navy blue cotton shorts and a matching t-shirt and went in search of gym shoes. After finding a pair, I stuffed my feet into them and scooped up my purse.

It was odd how all the front spots were always taken at Lakeview Gym. It was as if everybody thought that those extra few feet they would have to walk to get inside would kill them. Crazy. I parked in a different zip code, otherwise known as the last row, and made my way inside. After checking in at the front desk, I went straight to the women's locker room and locked up my purse.

My goal was forty minutes on the treadmill. I started at a slow walk and then began to run, an activity I personally loathed and despised, but it was a necessary evil. Supposedly, after a workout, people claimed to get these endorphin things. I thought they were full of crap. I bet they were just so lightheaded from living on carrots and sprouts that they only thought they felt good.

As punishment for the previous night's ice cream bender, I added an additional fifteen minutes onto my time. With a few minutes to go, I made the mistake of looking at the gentleman on my right side. He was dressed in a pair of way too short and tight navy blue shorts and a tank top. Blond hair, blue eyes, and eyelashes I would kill for. He smiled and I smiled back and I stumbled. Luckily I grabbed on and prevented myself from falling flat on my face. Only I could trip on a flat surface. Jeez.

"You should try cucumber slices for the bags under your eyes," he said.

"Thanks for the tip," I said, fully aware I hadn't asked his opinion. I hopped off the treadmill and walked back to the women's locker room. I got my stuff and headed home.

Back home, I went into the bathroom and looked at my face. I didn't think it looked *that* bad, but what did I know. I took my shower and got ready for work. Not wanting to match or clash with the purple in my office, I chose black shorts and a white t-shirt. I even put on makeup so as not to scare away any prospective clients.

I took everything I'd been working on for Aunt Tessa's case and headed out. After a trip through McDonald's drive-thru for a large coffee and a bacon, egg, and cheese biscuit, I headed to my office.

Inside, I flipped on the lights and got comfortable at my new desk. I christened it with my first breakfast and coffee. It felt good to be back. I even turned on the computer and checked my email. For some insane reason I had coupons for bungee jumping, skydiving, parasailing, zip line adventures, and even scuba diving lessons. I hated going above the third floor in buildings, I wasn't the greatest swimmer, and the thought of jumping out of a perfectly good airplane gave me nightmares. If they wanted to send me coupons I'd actually use, then they should send me ones for things like frozen yogurt, smoothies, and nail polish.

I finished my breakfast and opened the notebook to review the notes I'd been taking about Aunt Tessa's case. So far I hadn't learned much other than the dead guy had been a complete ass hat. I hated con artists. If they put half as much effort into a real job as they did into ripping people off, they would be wealthy and be able to sleep at night. I guessed that kind of scum slept fine despite what they did to innocent people.

I pulled out the flyer I had stuffed into my purse. Evidently, I could get a free quote for a new roof and siding. I pulled up the Better Business Bureau's website and plugged in their business name. It turned out they had quite a few locations. Each one had multiple complaints about getting ripped off. Mr. Patterson and his partners opened the location in Lakeview a few days after a storm had swept through with damaging winds and hail.

I dialed the number on the flyer and when a female voice answered the phone I asked to speak with Mr. Tipton. I was told that he was busy and was asked if I wanted to speak to one of the sales associates. I started to say no but ended up saying yes. I had no idea what I was going to say but decided to go with it.

"Hello, this is Kyle, how can I help you?"

I sat quietly for a few seconds while an idea brewed in my head. "Yes, I'd like a free inspection of my roof."

"Excellent. We can do that."

Over the next five minutes I answered questions about my possible need for a new roof. I gave him Melissa's address and my cell phone number. We set up an appointment for tomorrow morning. I thanked him and hung up. I still wasn't sure why I had done that, but whatever. I looked at the clock and decided it was several hours too early to call Melissa. I'd have to remember to call her later, so as not to just show up at her house unannounced and have people walking across her roof.

I figured it was late enough in the morning that I should be okay if I went door to door and asked the Pattersons' neighbors a few questions. I shut off my computer, tossed the food wrappers in the trash, and headed out to my car.

I parked at the opposite end of the street from where the Pattersons lived. I didn't think it wise to draw attention to my presence, not that the suddenly wealthy widow would recognize my car, but it was good to be cautious.

At the first house no one answered, so I moved on. The older woman who answered the door at the next house pointed to the *'No Soliciting'* sign and closed the door in my face without giving me a chance to explain my reason for being there.

At the third house, I lucked out a little bit, though when the teenage boy opened the door I hadn't thought so.

"Hi, are your parents home?" I asked.

"Nope." He brushed a strand of dishwater blond hair out of his eyes.

"Okay, well, I'm Kim Murphy. I'm a private investigator and I just wanted to ask a few questions about your neighbors, the Pattersons," I said.

"You mean the yellers? Yeah, I've seen them."

"The yellers?" I asked.

"Yeah, they fight all the time. I don't know how they could have that much to fight over. Though, I guess the little redhead is one reason."

"The little redhead?" I asked.

He leaned over and pointed down the street. "She lives two houses down from the Pattersons. Mr. Patterson seems to visit with her an awful lot."

"How do you know?"

"Sometimes at night, I climb out my window to sit on the roof and smoke some, I mean…" He stopped talking and covered his mouth with his hand.

"Relax, I'm not a cop. So, you hang out on your roof, chilling out, and you see what?"

"Mr. Patterson goes in the back door and stays inside for about a half an hour, then he goes back home."

"Wouldn't his wife notice?" I asked.

"Not unless she's awake at two in the morning," he replied.

"Oh. Okay. Well, is there anything else you can think of?"

"Nope."

"All right, well, thanks for your help." I handed him one of my business cards and asked him to call me if he thought of anything helpful. I said goodbye and walked toward the next house.

No answer at the next two homes. I left my business card, with a note on the back asking them to call me, taped to their front doors. I stepped up to the front door of the *little redhead* and tried my best to get rid of the hate. I had personal experience with a cheating spouse. In my professional life I spent hours following cheaters. I hated the cheating spouses and the idiots they hooked up with.

Envelopes were sticking out of the mailbox. I couldn't help myself. I lifted the lid and took a peek. All the mail was addressed to a Miss Barbara Greer. I stuffed the envelopes back in the mailbox before ringing the doorbell and waiting. The door opened and I plastered on a fake smile that felt like a grimace.

"Yes?" the red-haired young woman said.

Her eyes were red-rimmed, I assumed from crying. It wasn't easy to lose your lover, even if they already belonged to someone else.

"Are you Miss Greer?" I asked.

"Yes."

"Hello, my name is Kim Murphy. I'm a private investigator. I'm looking into the death of Derek Patterson. I was hoping you had a few minutes to speak with me."

She stared at me for a moment before bursting into tears. She turned around and headed back inside, leaving the door wide open. Considering that the only invitation I was going to get, I stepped inside and closed the door behind me.

I was standing in a too small foyer; all the furniture that had been stuffed into it—a cowhide love seat, a side table with now dead roses, and a bench. The walls were a bright red, like fresh blood, not the kind that had sat and been exposed to the air.

I followed the sound of sobbing, trying my best not to stare at the garish mix of Wild West meets urban modern. Sitting on a black leather couch was the woman who opened the door.

"I'm sorry for your loss," I said.

Miss Greer's head snapped up and she glared at me. "What are you doing in my house?" she asked.

"I wanted to see if you were all right," I lied.

"I'm fine." She grabbed a tissue from a box sitting next to her on the couch. She wiped her eyes and blew her nose. "You can go now," she said, tossing the crumpled up tissue into a pile of others.

"Actually, I need to ask you some questions about Mr. Patterson. Seeing as the two of you were so close," I said, watching for her reaction.

Her face turned red and she jumped up off the

couch. "I have no idea what you're insinuating but Derek was a friend. That was it."

"Really? Huh, my married male friends don't visit me in the middle of the night. They also don't play tongue hockey with me while standing at my back door," I said, adding the last bit to see if I could get her to confess.

She gasped. "Who told you?"

Got her. "That doesn't matter. What matters is your lover is dead. You seem upset, but who knows…"

"How dare you. Derek was a wonderful man."

"He must have been to have so many women mourning his loss."

"I don't know what you're talking about," she said.

"Don't you?"

"Look, we were in love. We were going to get married," she said.

"Did the two of you forget that he was already married?" I asked.

"Of course not. Derek was going to ask her for a divorce." She glared at me.

Derek had used the oldest line in the history of cheating spouses. Want to keep the piece on the side from wandering too far, dangle a happily ever after in their face. The more I learned about this guy, the happier I was that someone had killed him. Unfortunately, I still had to find his killer so I could clear Aunt Tessa.

"I'm sure he was. Can you tell me where you were when he was killed?" I asked.

"Oh my God. You think I killed him? I loved

him," she protested.

"People get murdered by loved ones all the time. Do you have an alibi or not?"

"I was home, alone."

"Can anyone corroborate that?" I asked.

"Huh?" she asked, crinkling her face.

I sighed. "Can anyone prove you were here?"

"No. How could I prove I was alone?"

It was a reasonable question, but I had a few more of my own. "What did you have for dinner that night?"

"What? I don't know."

I assumed with her two-inch acrylic nails, perfectly manicured, that she didn't spend a lot of time in the kitchen. "Did you cook or order takeout?" I asked, wondering if the five-foot talking skeleton with double Ds could lift her dead boyfriend's body.

"Oh God. I ordered Mexican for two. Derek was supposed to sneak over but he never showed. Now I know why." She burst into tears.

Dang it. As much as I really wanted her to be the killer, I was having doubts. Not that she wasn't capable; we all were if given the proper motivation. I just believed she really loved the guy and hadn't offed him. Now, if he had dumped her after promising to leave his wife, I could see her stabbing him or maybe even poisoning him, but to shoot him four times in the chest with a nail gun? I wasn't buying it, and that sucked—not for her but for Aunt Tessa.

"Do you happen to have the receipt?" I asked after she had gotten the sobbing under control.

"I...yes, I think so." She rushed out of the room and returned a few minutes later, waving a piece of paper in one hand and a Coach wallet in the other. She handed me the receipt. "See, I told you. I was here."

I didn't bother to tell her that all the receipt proved was that someone had signed for a food delivery. She could have signed for the food, killed Derek, and returned home without anyone noticing. I jotted down the name and phone number of the restaurant before handing the paper back to Barbara.

"So, what exactly did you tell the police?" I asked.

"I didn't tell them anything. Why should I?"

I tried to explain to her that she needed to come forward. After ten minutes I gave up. She wasn't budging, and to be honest, I couldn't blame her. It turned out no one from the police department had questioned her and she saw no reason to involve them now.

I knew there was another way to get that solved. I could go to the police myself. Not that I knew much but I needed to help Aunt Tessa. Sensing her patience with me was wearing thin, I gave Barbara my card and asked her to call me if she thought of anything else.

I spent the next couple of hours going door to door, careful to avoid the Pattersons' house, asking if anyone heard or saw anything the night Derek was killed. Either no one knew anything or wasn't willing to talk. I doled out a dozen more business cards and called it a day.

On the drive back to my office I called Melissa

and explained my crazy plan for tomorrow morning. As I'd suspected, she was up for it and eager to help in any way. I thanked her and hung up just as I pulled into the back parking lot.

I let myself into my office and headed straight for the kitchen. I made a pot of coffee, more out of habit than actual need, and sat down to make notes on what I'd learned so far. After I'd poured everything onto the notebook pages, I grabbed the file from Zack and sat with a cup of coffee and began to read.

An hour and two blurry eyes later, I looked up. I didn't see how Grant was able to arrest Aunt Tessa. So what if they had been in a dispute. If everyone went around killing people they were suing, the courts would be all freed up for actual criminal cases. Well, if you didn't count all the new murder cases, but whatever.

Besides, Aunt Tessa hadn't even recognized Derek Patterson. *Or had she?* the little annoying voice in my head asked. Aunt Tessa wouldn't have lied. She hadn't had any reason to. *Unless she did*, the voice insisted. I told it to shut up and tried to think of something else but failed. Not even surfing the web for pictures of horses, kittens, and puppies managed to get the stray thought out of my head.

The only way to make this go away was to talk to Aunt Tessa—alone. No family and no lawyer. Sorry, Zack, but it had to be done. Before I could talk myself out of it, I picked up the phone and called her. She answered on the third ring.

"Hello."

"Aunt Tessa, hi, it's Kim."

"Kim, how are you?" she asked.

"I'm fine. I was wondering if we could talk for a few minutes, just the two of us."

"Of course. I'm all by my lonesome right now. The girls are coming over for dinner. Why don't you join us? I'm making my famous jambalaya."

I told her I'd be right over. I didn't say anything about the dinner invitation because I wasn't sure I'd still be welcome there after our little chat. I took my empty mug into the kitchen and spent a few minutes tidying things up, otherwise known as stalling. When I was done I got my purse, shut off my computer and the lights, and locked up.

Fifteen minutes later I pulled up in front of Aunt Tessa's house. I walked up the driveway and rang the doorbell. Aunt Tessa opened the door with her hair and makeup done, wearing a red dress, heels, and some pretty impressive diamonds on her fingers and around her neck. She looked ready for a night on the town except for the apron with the words *'Keep Calm and Cook On'* covering her dress.

"Kim, come on in."

I stepped inside and closed the door behind me. I followed her down the hall and into the kitchen where the smell invaded my senses and I suddenly realized I was starving. My stomach growled but I silently urged it to stop. I rolled my tongue back into my mouth and realized that Aunt Tessa was talking.

"And I told her there was no way I was giving her my mother's recipe."

Unsure of how to respond to a conversation I hadn't participated in, I smiled and nodded.

"So, what was it you wanted to discuss? I'm pretty sure you didn't come all this way to hear about my mother's recipes," Aunt Tessa said.

"You said you didn't recognize Derek Patterson, but he lived in your neighborhood, his face was on all those signs, and, well, you were suing him."

Aunt Tessa picked up a white plastic spoon and began tapping it against her leg. "Kim, I was being truthful. I didn't recognize him. Not then anyway."

"When did you recognize him?" I asked.

The spoon stopped in mid-swing and Aunt Tessa looked me in the eye. "At the police station when that detective was questioning me."

Of course Grant had asked her if she recognized the dead guy; after all, his body was found in her yard not once but twice. Which still didn't make any sense to me. I mean, if you went through the trouble to kill someone, why relocate the body just to move it back again?

"Kim…"

"Huh? Sorry, just thinking. What did you tell Grant, I mean, Detective Tompkins?"

"I told him the truth. That it hadn't dawned on me until later that he was one of the men on the signs for the company I was suing."

"Why are you suing them?" I asked.

"Someone from his company came out and claimed I needed a new roof after that storm we had. Well, I signed that stupid estimate and the next thing I know I've agreed to pay them fifteen thousand dollars for a new roof."

"What?"

"Yeah. Then, since I was stuck, I paid them half

down, but then no one ever showed up to do the work. Then they started refusing my calls. That's when I contacted my lawyer."

"Assholes," I said.

"Yes, but here's the worst part. I had my cousin's son take a look at it. Turns out I didn't need a new roof after all. I was furious. I'd been scammed out of a lot of money." She slapped the spoon onto the stove. "But that doesn't mean I killed anybody over it."

"I'm sorry you're going through all this," I said.

"Me too, but it could be worse. So, I'll just keep praying." She grabbed my hands and smiled. "I'm sure the good Lord will see me through. And I just know He's going to help you find a way out of this. So, in a way, you're doing the Lord's work."

I didn't think God would appreciate that logic but I let it go. Before I could come up with a response, Charmaine and Shandra walked into the room.

"Girl, what are you doin' here?" Charmaine asked.

Shandra looked at me and frowned.

Aunt Tessa looked at me and smiled. "She's here to have dinner with us. Is that my mail?" she asked, pointing to the stack of envelopes in Charmaine's hand.

"Yeah, most of it is. The rest is supposed to go to Fernmont. You'd think the mail carrier could read the difference between Fernmont and Ferndale. Jeez."

"It happens all the time. Just set it over there," Aunt Tessa said, pointing at a metal rack on the wall. "I'll sort it later."

Charmaine did as asked then walked over to the stove and picked up a spoon.

"Don't even think about it, young lady. Wash your hands and set the table."

"Yes, ma'am."

As soon as Charmaine left the room, Shandra asked me if everything was all right.

"Everything is fine. Now, take these glasses and go help your sister," Aunt Tessa replied before I could say anything.

Shandra looked at her aunt and back at me. "Okay." With one last glare at me, she left the room.

Despite the unease, at least on my part, and a bit on Shandra's, dinner was fun and delicious. Afterward, I tried to help clear the table but Aunt Tessa wouldn't hear of it.

"Sit and relax."

Charmaine turned and winked at me before facing her aunt. "So, how come the skinny white girl doesn't have to help?"

Aunt Tessa glared at Charmaine. "How many times have you eaten a meal at the Murphy's house?"

"Hundreds of times. Why?"

"Have you lifted a single glass or plate while over there?"

"No, but so what?" Charmaine said.

"A guest will help with dishes in this house only after I'm dead and gone. Now get *your* not so skinny ass up and help me," Aunt Tessa said.

I clapped my hand over my mouth. Shandra

151

laughed while Charmaine did her best to look and sound indignant until she burst out laughing. I passed on the offer of dessert. No offense to Aunt Tessa but key lime pie was one of my least favorite foods. We said our goodbyes and I got in my car and drove to the nearest pharmacy. Inside I bought a six-pack of beer and a package of Reese's Pieces, M&M's, and a Hershey's Bar.

At home, I walked toward the back door and froze when I spotted Grant sitting in a chair on my back patio, which was only slightly larger than a DVD case. With Grant there it somehow appeared even smaller. Grant smiled and raised a can of beer, as if in tribute, before putting it to his lips. I began to walk toward the patio when I noticed his disheveled appearance. Normally, Grant's suits and ties were wrinkle and stain free, while this one looked like he'd slept in it. His hair looked like he'd run his hands through it a few too many times. At the thought, my own fingers ached to run through it as well. Plus, if I was honest, there were plenty other far more interesting places they longed to touch.

I stepped onto the porch and noticed the empty beer cans scattered around his chair. It seemed he'd been waiting for me for a while. I raised my own pack of beer up so he could see. "Great minds think alike," I said.

Grant smiled. "Good idea, but you're gonna have to catch up," he said, pointing to the empty cans littering the concrete slab that was my patio.

"Bad day?" I asked as I sat across from him.

"Yup," he said, reaching for one of my beers

152

when he discovered his were all empty.

I didn't bother to ask if he wanted to talk about it. I knew that one word was all the answer I would get, but that was okay. I was pretty sure I didn't want the details. A bad day for a homicide cop wasn't something I really wanted to think about. Especially if I wanted to be able to sleep without a nightlight tonight or ever again.

We sat in silence and drank. Well, Grant drank and drank while I nursed the one can. I figured it was best if one of us stayed sober, and since it was too late for him, I was it.

Grant reached for another can of beer. Not finding one, he stood up.

"Where are you going?" I asked, jumping up and blocking the exit.

"To get more beer."

His speech was slurred and he was wobbling from side to side. Unlike the odd little toy I'd played with as a child, I had no hope Grant wouldn't fall down. I leaned forward and held onto his arm.

"More beer? Great idea." I turned him around so we were facing the sliding doors. "I've got a case in the fridge," I lied.

"Awethom."

After several failed attempts, I was finally able to open the door and get him inside. The single step up had been a real bitch but we did it and I'd only suffered a minor scrape when I'd bashed the side of my face into the doorframe.

It was slow going but I got him to the front of the couch, and just in time. I let go for just a second and he landed face down with a thud.

"Grant, are you okay?"

"Hmm," was his muffled reply.

Relieved he'd survived the fall, I went back outside and collected all the empty beer cans. I tossed them into the recycling bin before locking up the door. I walked back in the living room and smiled. In my brief absence, Grant had managed to wiggle around and had curled up in the fetal position.

As I stared at him I began to frown. In all fairness, in his current disheveled appearance, Grant should look like crap, like I would. Instead, he looked vulnerable, and about as sexy as Channing Tatum and Matt Bomer in the *Magic Mike* movie I'd insisted, I mean, been forced to watch, five times.

Grant looked up at me and frowned. "Why are you on the ceiling?"

I smiled. "Go to sleep."

"Okay."

I leaned down and picked up a blanket I kept folded over the back of the couch. As I tucked him in, he closed his eyes, smiled, and whispered, "I love you."

I sucked in a breath, stumbled backward, and banged the side of my knee into the coffee table. I covered my mouth with my hand so as not to wake him. I was sure he hadn't meant what he'd said. A part of me was relieved, but the other part was disappointed.

I had no idea how long I stood there watching him sleep, but eventually, exhausted, I climbed the stairs, and after a few minutes in the bathroom, I stripped out of my clothes and crawled under the covers.

CHAPTER NINE

I opened my eyes and squinted. The sun was rudely announcing its presence by shining brightly into my window. I rolled over and looked at the alarm clock. I couldn't believe it was almost ten o'clock. I'd gone to bed so early.

Of course just the thought of Grant sleeping downstairs on my couch had been enough to cause sleep to be evasive. The last time I'd checked the clock it had been a little after three. I got out of bed and rushed around getting ready. As I was cutting it close I didn't bother with drying my hair. I went downstairs and discovered my couch was empty except for a folded up blanket.

Since I didn't have time to think about why that caused me to be so sad, I left out the back door and blasted the radio once I got inside the car. I arrived at Melissa's with ten minutes to spare. I punched in the security code and waited for the gate to open. I drove up the tree-lined drive and parked my car in front of the garage. Melissa opened the front door as I walked up the front steps.

156

"Cutting it kind of close, aren't you?" Melissa asked.

"Sorry, long night."

"Oh, really? Do tell." She smiled as I walked past her.

"Insomnia," I replied.

"Ooh, how boring."

"Sorry my life isn't exciting enough for you," I said.

"That's all right. We'll just have to liven it up a bit."

Melissa's ideas were about as bad as one of Fred's traps on *Scooby-Doo*. I'd lived through them and still had some of the scars to prove it. Like the one on my knee that looked like a circle. We were eight and Melissa had convinced me that we could ride Michael and Brandon's bikes. She'd been right at first. Encouraged by our success, I followed her down Pleasant Hill Drive. Halfway down, I crashed and ended up with a rock imbedded in my knee.

Being a true friend, she'd raced back to my house to get help. She'd even stayed with me and held my hand while the doctor stitched up my knee. That was until she made the mistake of looking at my leg. One look at the blood and down she went. Luckily my mom caught Melissa just before her head hit the floor. She ended up in the hospital bed next to mine. We were there for several hours before we were finally released.

Melissa looked at me. "Shouldn't you have dressed up a little? I mean, jeans? What were you thinking?" she asked.

I glanced down at myself and realized in my rush

157

to get here I hadn't considered my wardrobe choices; not that there were really too many things to choose from, but I really hadn't thought this through.

"So? You wear jeans too."

"Yes, but they're designer jeans. Plus, what is going on with your hair?" Melissa asked.

"I didn't have time to dry it. Does it look that bad?"

"No, but you really should run upstairs and run a brush through it."

"Fine." I stomped off down the hall and into one of the six bathrooms. I glanced in the mirror and groaned at my reflection. Melissa was right. In my current state, no one would believe I was the homeowner of an estate worth almost two million dollars. I brushed my hair and grimaced. Though I looked much better, I still wasn't estate worthy. I walked back down the hall and stopped as I entered the foyer. Melissa was standing where I'd left her, only now she wasn't alone. Standing in front of her were two men with dark hair wearing blue Oxford-style shirts with their company's logo on the left breast pocket.

"Gentlemen, I'd like to introduce you to my assistant, Kim. She'll be following along in case I have any questions."

"Of course. No trouble at all." The one closest to me turned and smiled. "How do you do? I'm Tom from Ohio's Premier Ace Roofing Company, and this is David. He's a new trainee."

I smiled and shook Tom's extended hand. David smiled and I nodded in his general direction. The four of us walked out the front door. Outside, Melissa and I followed behind the two men, listening to their mumbo jumbo about how hard this last storm had been on all the roofs and how wonderful their company was.

Melissa walked around like the lady of the manor, which of course she was, but that made me the help, and that was an all too familiar feeling I had whenever I was around some of Zack's friends. Not that I'd spent much time with them over the years. After one nasty incident in high school, I avoided them all. Well, except for Michael of course. Though sometimes I would like to avoid my brother, all such attempts usually failed.

After circling the whole house, Tom informed us he and David would be getting their ladders and inspecting the roof. They would ring the doorbell when they were done. Melissa thanked them and we went back inside. Though it was only ten o'clock it was already turning out to be a scorcher. I was thrilled to be back inside with the air conditioning but instantly felt sorry for the two men who would soon be walking around on Melissa's roof.

Back inside, Melissa led the way to one of her favorite rooms in the house, the solarium. I'd never understood why she'd needed such a room. Almost every plant or flower I had been entrusted with managed to go from healthy, thriving specimen to dead and decaying within a matter of hours.

The first time Melissa had insisted on bringing me in here, I had reminded her of the horrendous deaths numerous fauna had suffered at my hands, but she'd assured me her flowers were perfectly

159

safe. I hadn't been as sure and had been extra careful to avoid touching anything while I'd been inside. Over the past few years, I'd been in the room numerous times and so far none of Melissa's glorious roses had suffered the same fate as my own.

To be safe, like always, I chose the chair closest to the doorway. While we waited for the roofing guys we chatted about not much of anything. Melissa told me about her most recent book. As soon as she was happy with it I'd get to read it before her publisher got to see it. I wasn't sure why I got it first since I was of no help at all. I could tell her what I liked and if it worked but that was about it.

She was just about to tell me about the bad guy when the doorbell rang. We got up and walked to the front of the house. Before she opened the door, I reminded her not to sign anything. She assured me she was fine and plastered on a smile.

It seemed that Tom had *discovered* several holes in Melissa's roof. The damage was so severe that she needed a whole new roof right away. As I'd predicted, Tom tried his best to get Melissa to sign her *free estimate*.

"I'm sorry, but I won't be signing anything today. Just leave a copy with me and I will discuss it with my insurance company," Melissa said.

"But if you don't sign it now, you won't qualify for the ten percent discount," Tom insisted.

"That's all right. I can afford to pay full price." She took a copy and handed it to me before handing Tom the other copy. "Thank you so much for your time." He tried again to persuade her but Melissa held firm, closing and then locking the door.

"Wow. Thanks, Melissa."

"No problem. I don't like pushy salesmen. If that's how they treat all perspective clients, it's no wonder someone murdered one of the owners," Melissa said.

"Yikes. You might want to keep that to yourself," I said.

"Good point."

I glanced down at the paper in my hand. "Oh my gosh, thirty thousand dollars. Are they insane?"

"They'd have to be. It only cost me half that when I had the new one installed a few months ago. Actually, because of the winter storm we had, insurance covered all but a thousand dollars."

"So they convince people who don't need new roofs that they need one, plus they have them sign what looks like an estimate but is really a contract, and on top of all of that they are price gouging and take your money and don't finish the work or do a half-ass job."

"Sounds about right," Melissa said.

"I've changed my mind. I'm surprised it took this long for someone to kill one of them."

"The guy was scum. Maybe the killer did the world a favor. You might not want to look too hard for him or her."

"Did you forget about Aunt Tessa?" I asked.

"Oh, that. No way did she kill him. She's innocent and I know you'll prove it."

I didn't bother to point out to her the contradiction. I told her I was leaving and thanked her for her help.

"You can't go yet."

"I have to get to the office," I said.

"No, I got this new foot bath stuff that promises to remove all the toxins from your body. Doesn't that sound wonderful?"

"Uh, sure," I lied. "Sorry, maybe another time."

It took a few minutes and a sincere promise to return to try the dreaded foot bath before I was able to escape. On my way to the office I went through a fast food drive-thru and ordered more toxins, I mean, lunch, and sat at my desk to enjoy every bite.

I was enjoying the last of the french fries when I looked up and spotted Mrs. Patterson dressed in black pants and blouse standing in my doorway. I swallowed, said hello, and motioned for her to come inside.

"Thank you." She walked over and sat down in one of the chairs across from my desk. "I'm sorry to bother you, especially during your lunch. I just didn't know where else to go," Mrs. Patterson said.

"That's all right. What can I do for you?" I asked, hoping whatever it was would be over quickly.

She opened and closed her mouth several times. Finally, she reached into her purse, pulled out a picture, and slid it across my desk. I picked it up and she burst into tears. "I want to know who *that* woman is and what she was doing with my husband."

I stared at the picture and frowned. I was staring at an apparent selfie of the late Mr. Patterson wrapped in the arms of a certain redhead.

I knew firsthand the pain of finding out my husband was a lying, cheating ass. The difference was mine was still alive and kicking, despite the overwhelming urge I'd had to chop him into small pieces and bury him in the backyard.

As horrible as I'd felt, I wouldn't trade places with Mrs. Patterson. Yesterday she was grieving the loss of her husband. Today, she had started grieving the loss of her marriage. She couldn't ask him why he'd been banging the redheaded bimbo. Not that there was any excuse. I hadn't listened to my ex when he'd tried to be logical. He'd been fortunate I hadn't gone after him with my grandmother's cast iron skillet or my grandfather's Smith & Wesson.

I looked up from the picture and watched Mrs. Patterson dab at her eyes with a wadded up tissue. There was absolutely nothing I could say that would give her any peace of mind. Some days my job really sucked.

"I'm sorry, Mrs. Patterson. I know this must be a difficult time for you," I said.

"Yes, it is. I loved my husband. I don't understand this. Who is she? What was he doing with her?"

Instead of answering her questions, I stood up and hoped she would follow suit. She glanced up at me and frowned. "Well?"

Much to my utter disappointment, she wasn't taking the hint. She looked ready to stay as long as it took to get answers. I just hoped she was prepared for whatever she heard. Especially since I wasn't sure exactly what I was going to say. I had to be careful not to offend her or her love for the recently departed, even if he was scum. He'd been her scum, and despite her suspicions, that didn't make the love suddenly disappear like a magician's assistant. No, the love lingered, which forced the pain to hang around much longer than seemed fair.

"Mrs. Patterson. I'm sure you have so much to do. Isn't there anyone you could call to be at home with you?" I sat back down at my desk and picked up a pencil. I began tapping it against the desk while I waited for her to respond.

She straightened herself up in the chair, her head tilted slightly to the left. She took several deep breaths before speaking. "My mom will arrive tomorrow." She raised a hand and brushed a strand of hair away from her face. "Please, Miss Murphy. I need answers."

Seeing the hurt and confusion in her eyes, I hesitated. Finally, I plunged ahead with the band-aid method. "Your late husband was having an affair with the woman in the photo. I've already spoken with her. She claims Mr. Patterson was going to leave you for her."

I watched as her face contorted from shock, to rage, and finally settled on disbelief.

"No way. She's lying."

Knowing there was no point in arguing with her, I remained silent.

"It isn't possible. He'd finally agreed we could start trying to get pregnant. We threw my birth control pills in the trash and celebrated with a bottle of wine and some fabulous strawberries and cream."

"I'm sorry," I said.

She stared at me and burst into tears. I waited

until she was finally able to get herself under control. "I just don't understand how he could have done this. Why? Why would he make plans for a future with me if he was seeing that slut on the side? I need to talk to her."

Since I didn't want to be dragged in as an accessory to murder, I refused to give her the woman in the picture's name or contact information. Mrs. Patterson stood up and shouted, "I have a right to know who she is!"

"That's not a good idea."

"It isn't your choice to make. I need to know how this happened." She picked the picture up from the desk and thrust it at me. "I need to know."

I felt bad for her, but not enough to put another woman in danger, even if that *other* woman was a husband-stealing skank. "I'll make you a deal. Make a list of the questions you want answers to, and I'll ask her."

She shook her head *no* and opened her mouth. I raised my hand to ward off whatever argument she was about to start. "Take it or leave it, but I'm not giving you her name."

The two of us sat in silence for several minutes. Just as I was convinced she was never going to get her ass out of my office, she agreed. I told her to come back tomorrow with her list and I'd have the answers for her in a few days. She pulled her checkbook from her purse. I waved it away.

"This is free of charge."

"That isn't fair. I should at least pay for a couple of hours of your time."

Eager to get her out of my office, I once again

stood up and was much relieved when she did also.

"Thank you, Miss Murphy." She took my hand and shook it, then followed me to the front door. I was grateful and a bit surprised when she didn't say anything about my speed walking all the way down the hall.

I opened the door and she walked past me to leave. "Mrs. Patterson, did you know about the trouble with your husband's company?" I asked.

"What trouble? He was a roofer."

"Never mind. I'll see you."

"Tomorrow?" she asked.

"Absolutely."

I closed and locked the door behind her. I went into the kitchen and looked around for something to clean. Whenever I was stuck or stalling, I tended to do mundane household chores to take my mind off whatever it was that was bothering me. Sadly, with the office newly remodeled, there was nothing for me to do.

I couldn't even go home and tidy up because I'd already done that. I felt a sudden craving for chocolate. I scrounged around the entire kitchen and office and came up with nothing. I scooped up my keys and my purse, making sure to lock the door and set the alarm.

I drove down the street and turned into Beth's Bakery. I parked between a white Hummer and a red Porsche. As I walked toward the door, a black Lexus pulled into the lot. The little bakery was always busy. That was thanks to Beth's magical ways with cakes, pies, and cookies. Her competition swore she'd made a deal with the Devil. It was the only way they could explain Beth's delectable creations. Personally, I didn't care what she'd done, as long as I could get chocolate cupcakes with buttercream frosting, which after waiting in line for ten minutes, was exactly what I did.

I got to my car and ate the first one. Then the second one just sat there in the box, taunting me. So, I did what any reasonable woman would do...I ate it too. I was about to head back to the office but I was feeling a bit guilty about all the junk food and all-too-frequent desserts. Deciding to make amends, I put the car in gear and headed for Lakeview Gym.

Once inside, I spent twenty minutes jogging in place on a treadmill. Still feeling kind of yucky, I changed into a bathing suit and headed for the pool. My initial plan was to simply enjoy the water for a while before heading home and making myself a salad. I ended up doing laps for fifteen minutes, hoping to avoid the hated, soon-to-be divorced and future bride-to-be Maria Gonzalez-Feldman.

It seemed one of her offspring was taking a swim class and she actually was here instead of pawning it off on one of the nannies. Just as I was beginning to fear the lesson would never end, Maria's lovely little girl got out of the pool and headed straight for her mom. Of course, instead of paying attention to her daughter, Maria was glued to the phone. Finally getting her mother's attention, the little girl led the way to the locker room. Fearing my skin would be permanently wrinkled, I jumped out of the pool and wrapped myself in a towel.

I waited about twenty minutes before venturing into the locker room. I scanned the room and let out a sigh of relief when the evil bitch who tortured me in high school was nowhere to be found. Granted, I didn't think she'd resort to violence in front of her daughter, but I wasn't really interested in finding out.

She'd been a cheerleader, along with my sister, and had hated me on sight. She had fallen hard for Zack and despised the fact that he ignored her and always paid attention to me. Whenever she tried to embarrass me, he'd always risen to my defense. When she hadn't been able to lure him into her web, or rather, bed, she'd gone on a mission—destroy Kim.

If not for Melissa, Charmaine, and Shandra, the slut may have been successful. After one particularly nasty bout of vengeance, they had hatched a plan. The next day we all changed into our shorts and t-shirts and went into the gym. Charmaine had faked a sudden need to run to the restroom. Once inside the locker room she had stolen Maria's clothes and tossed them in the bottom of the trash can, covering them up with toilet paper and paper towels. After gym class we all traipsed back into the locker room to change clothes before heading home.

It all seemed so normal until Maria started screaming. Of course, she immediately accused me of having done something to her clothes, but as the gym teacher pointed out, I hadn't been in the room alone and the locker was still locked when we entered the room. Of course Maria locked onto my friends next but there was not a single shred of evidence against them, so the gym teacher let it drop.

I'd always hated cold weather, but that day it was such a wonderful surprise to see it had snowed three inches while we'd been forced to run laps and chase after a stupid ball. Maria had been forced to ride the bus home in her shorts, t-shirt, and winter coat. Even now the image managed to bring a smile to my face.

I looked up and saw Maria walk through the other entrance. Shit. I spun around and threw my clothes on over my suit. I grabbed my purse and escaped through the entrance that led back to the pool. I didn't breathe a sigh of relief until I was safely ensconced in my car.

Back home, I stripped out of my clothes and was just about to get out of the purple bikini when the doorbell rang. I wrapped a towel around me and raced down the stairs. I opened the door and found Grant standing on my front step. He was back to his immaculate appearance in a black suit and tie. His hair was neat and orderly, even if it did need a trim. He looked me up and down, a slow smile playing with his lips.

"Grant, what are you doing here?" I asked.

"I wanted to talk to you. If you're not busy," he said, frowning.

"Come on in." I stepped aside to let him in. His arm brushed against my breast, causing both nipples to tighten. I looked down and groaned. That would be a bit difficult to hide in a swimsuit and towel. I closed the door and turned around, but not before I folded my arms over my chest.

"Going somewhere?" he asked pointing to my

outfit.

"No, I just got back from doing laps at the pool."

Grant smiled. "So, what exactly do you have on under that towel?"

"I guess you'll have to find out," I said.

"Good idea." He pulled me against him, trapping my arms between our bodies.

"Grant, I…"

"Shh." He leaned down and brushed his lips against my forehead. I opened my mouth to tell him I was sorry but his tongue slipped inside and took full possession. His hands began to roam everywhere. My own ached to touch him.

Grant tore his lips from mine. "I want you," he whispered in my ear, sending shivers up and down my body. Unable to speak, all I could do was nod. Grant scooped me up in his arms and carried me up the stairs. He set me down on the bed. "Take off the towel." I did and his eyes scanned over me from head to toe. "Very nice, but I much prefer you naked."

***

It was ten o'clock and we had managed to work up quite an appetite. I ordered pizza, salad, and breadsticks from Cousin Lou's Pizzeria. Over dinner we stuck to small talk like the weather and sports. Since my knowledge of sports was limited, he did all the talking. I wasn't sure if he was nervous or uncomfortable but I felt a little awkward. I didn't like that but I wasn't sure how to fix it.

After dinner, we cleaned up the paper plates and

empty food containers. Once everything was put away, I made sure the doors were locked and Grant followed me upstairs. We stripped out of our clothes and crawled under the covers. Grant pulled me against him. Sometime later I fell asleep.

"Wake up," Grant said.

"No." I rolled over and hid under the covers.

"Someone is at the door."

"What?" I sat up straight. "What time is it?"

"It's nine o'clock."

"Who the hell visits that early?" I asked.

"Most people have been up for hours."

"I'm not most people," I said.

"I've noticed."

I got out of bed and pulled on the nearest clothes, which happened to be a pair of jeans and a *Star Wars* t-shirt. I ran downstairs and looked out the peephole. On the other side of the door were two gentlemen dressed in dark suits and ties. Just great.

I opened the door and plastered on a fake smile. "Yes?"

"Hello, are you Kimberly Murphy?" the one with blond hair asked.

"Yes."

"Wonderful. My name is George Brown, and this is my husband, William Snider-Brown," he said, pointing to the man with dark hair and eyes.

"Hello."

"We're your new neighbors," he said, pointing to the once empty apartment next door to mine.

"That's great. Welcome to the neighborhood."

"Thank you." George glanced over at William and back at me.

171

"Was there something else?" I asked.

"Well…"

Grant walked over and stood next to me. "Is everything okay?" Grant asked.

"Yup. I think." I turned back toward George. "What was it you wanted to say?"

George cleared his throat. "Well, you see, it seems the walls in this place aren't as thick as I'd hoped and well…oh dear. I'm afraid your vociferous lovemaking was extremely disconcerting."

"Excuse me?"

"We didn't get much sleep last night. So, we'd appreciate it if you could keep it down."

Grant laughed and I elbowed him in the ribs. "Sure thing."

"Wonderful."

Mortified, I closed the door in their faces and turned around. "Wipe that stupid grin off your face."

"Nope."

"Jackass," I said as I tried to brush past him.

Grant grabbed me and pulled me against him. "I'd love to stay and continue this but I've got to get to a crime scene."

"Lucky you."

"Dinner tonight?" he asked.

"Yeah, especially if you're buying."

"Sure. How about Mexican?"

"That sounds great."

Grant leaned down and lingered over a kiss. Before I could insist we head back upstairs, he pulled away, said goodbye, and left out the front door. In my bedroom, I considered getting ready for work but the bed beckoned me. I crawled under the covers and closed my eyes.

It was ten thirty the next time I opened my eyes. I climbed out of bed, stripped out of my clothes, and jumped into the shower. Forty minutes later I was on my way to the office. I made a quick detour through the McDonald's drive-thru for a double cheeseburger, large fries, and a large Diet Coke.

After parking the car and letting myself in through the back door, I flipped on lights and headed straight for my office, where I sat at my desk to eat lunch. I made the mistake of glancing at the phone. The number four was flashing. Instead of listening to the messages, I turned on the computer and checked email and the local news. Then I went to an online dictionary and looked up the word vociferous. I closed out the page and turned my attention to my food. Once I was done eating I turned my attention to the messages.

The first one was from Melissa, asking me to call her, but not until after five. The next three were from Mrs. Patterson. I deleted the messages and was just about to return Mrs. Patterson's calls when the phone rang.

"Hello, Murphy Investigations, how may I help you?" I asked.

"Oh, thank goodness. Miss Murphy, it's me, Mrs. Patterson."

"I was just about to call you. How can I help you?" I asked.

"I'm on my way to your office now. I have that list of questions for that tramp, I mean, the woman who was sleeping with my husband. I was hoping you could speak with her today."

"I'll do my best. I can't promise she'll cooperate," I said, wishing I hadn't agreed to do this.

"That's all right. Just do your best. I'll see you in a few," she said, and hung up.

I dumped the wrappers from my lunch in the trash and did a quick scan to see if I'd managed to spill food on my jeans or t-shirt. I was pleasantly surprised to find no traces of McDonald's on my clothes. I walked to the front and unlocked the door. I'd just made it back to my office when I heard someone knock. I walked back and found Mrs. Patterson, still all in black, pacing back and forth.

"Please come in," I said.

"Thank you."

Mrs. Patterson followed me down the hall. Once inside my office, I offered her a seat as I took my own. She pulled a piece of paper from her purse and slid it across the desk. I picked it up and silently went over the surprisingly short list of questions. I was pretty sure I'd have more than that, but then again, I was a bit odd.

"That's it?" I asked her, making sure she hadn't forgotten anything.

"Yes. I'm sure I'll feel so much better. I would give anything for a good night's sleep," Mrs. Patterson said.

I didn't have the heart to tell her having the

answers wouldn't improve her chances of getting a full night's sleep. She wouldn't listen to me anyway. This was one of those things you just had to learn for yourself. She didn't need me to tell her that the answers could end up leading to even more questions. Which in turn led to more pain and even more anger—at least in my case it had. The only thing that had prevented me from taking a crowbar to my ex's head was the shared toilet, out in the open for everyone to see, in the prison cells. That was just beyond disgusting.

I glanced over and realized she was waiting for me to say something. I smiled. "I'll do what I can. Don't worry too much about this. You can't change what happened. All you can do now is move forward," I said.

Mrs. Patterson stood up. "I know you're right. I just can't imagine being the talk of the neighborhood."

"I'm sure it isn't like that," I tried to reassure her, knowing full well that it was exactly like that.

"Do you have any idea who killed my husband?" she asked.

"No, I'm sorry, I don't."

"Damn. I was hoping you had arrested someone."

There were so many things wrong with that. First, I couldn't arrest anyone, other than a citizen's arrest, and our local police department wasn't a big fan. Second, someone had already been arrested, Aunt Tessa. I was just grateful Mrs. Patterson didn't seem to think Aunt Tessa had done it either. Too bad her opinion wouldn't hold up in court. I was pretty sure there was a third reason, but for the life of me I just couldn't remember what it was. Sigh.

Mrs. Patterson thanked me and said she would call tomorrow. After she left I plotted out my plans for the rest of the day. It didn't take long. I had hoped to have some idea who had killed her husband. Not just for her sake but most especially for Aunt Tessa. I sat and thought about ways I could avoid asking the slut questions, but in a moment of weakness I had made a promise to a woman struggling with loss and betrayal. I felt for her.

I spent an hour at my desk surfing the web for discount name brand purses. In the end I decided I just couldn't buy a purse online. I had to look at it and touch it to get a sense of if we would be a good match. Besides, if it wasn't big enough to hold my wallet, a can of mace, my Glock, and a myriad of other items, then it would have to go back, and that would just suck.

Having stalled for as long as I could, I shut the computer off, saying a goodbye to a particularly awesome Anne Klein purse in beige. I picked up my no-name purse and keys and locked up.

I drove to the Pattersons' neighborhood. Out of habit I started to turn onto Aunt Tessa's street. I quickly altered my course, earning a horn blast for my last second direction change. I turned onto the Pattersons' street and drove past their house. A white Porsche sat in Mrs. Patterson's driveway. I was grateful it was empty. The last thing I needed was for her to see me in her neighborhood. It wouldn't take her long to figure out the woman who'd been sleeping with her husband was also a neighbor. Yikes.

I parked on the street, three doors down from the redhead's house, and walked back. I knocked on the door and waited for the woman I imagined with a scarlet letter on her face. She opened the door and frowned.

"What are you doing here?" Barbara asked.

"Why, it's so good to see you too," I said.

She started to close the door but I stuck my foot in the doorframe.

"What the hell are you doing?"

"I just need a few minutes of your time," I said.

"I have nothing to say to you," Barbara said.

"Too bad. We need to talk."

"About what?"

"Derek." With that one word a dam broke. Barbara burst into tears. I really had to learn to be more cautious about my word choices. I stepped inside and closed the door behind me. I took Barbara's arm and guided her through the house. Somehow we ended up in the kitchen.

A part of me felt sorry for her. Yes, she was the other woman, but she'd lost the man she loved. The widow would get help and support. Not so much for the girl on the side. Granted, she'd fallen for a man who already belonged to someone else, but her pain was real.

Barbara took a seat at the table. I glanced around the room and nearly jumped when a loud whistling noise began. I spun around and spotted the culprit—a tea kettle on the gas stove. With the invention of the microwave, I didn't understand why people still used a kettle. I walked over and turned off the burner. Barbara had placed a mug with a tea bag inside on the counter. I filled it with water, walked over to the table, and handed it to her.

She looked up at me through her tears and managed a smile. She even croaked out a thank you. We sat in silence. The only sound was Barbara taking sips of her tea. Once she got herself under control, she asked me what I needed to talk to her about.

"I'm afraid Mrs. Patterson found a picture of you and her husband. She's asking questions."

"Oh no, I just can't deal with that. Not now. Ever since I found out about…I can't sleep, I'm sick to my stomach. I made coffee this morning and the smell made me sick. What could she possibly want to know?" Barbara asked.

"Things like, how did the two of you meet, when did the affair begin, did you ever have sex in her house?"

"Oh Lord. Why does she want to know all that?"

"Wouldn't you want to know?" I asked instead of answering her question.

"I guess. I don't know. I hadn't thought about it." Barbara set her mug on the table and began rubbing at her temples. "This is just horrible."

It was, so I just sat there silently waiting.

"We met at a neighbor's yard sale. We were both admiring the same stupid painting. He offered to let me have it if I agreed to have dinner with him." She smiled but didn't really see me. "He was funny and gorgeous. Of course I said yes. I didn't find out he was married until after we'd," she looked at me and blushed, "uh, slept together."

"Why didn't you end things when you found out he was married?" I asked.

"Because I loved him. Shaina was always pressuring him."

"How do you know?"

She sighed. "Derek told me." She tapped her fingers on the table. "He didn't make enough money, he didn't spend enough time with her, he didn't listen to her."

"That's a lot of arguing. I can't figure out why she was so desperate to have a baby with him," I said, more to myself than to Barbara.

"What?"

"Shaina told me Derek had finally agreed to try to get pregnant," I said.

"Why? Why would he do that?" Barbara jumped up and started pacing the room. "He was going to leave her. We were going to get married, start a family. I told him about the pregnancy test the day before he disappeared."

Oh shit. "You're pregnant?" I asked.

"About eight weeks," she replied, placing her hand on her flat belly. "What are the baby and I going to do without Derek?" she asked, bursting into another round of tears.

I waited until she got her crying under control before asking her what Derek's response to the baby news had been.

"He was surprised at first but he was thrilled.

He said he'd tell Shaina and that we could finally be together."

So, his something on the side got pregnant while his wife was trying to get pregnant. I bet the man was surprised. I'd say shocked was a natural reaction to that kind of news. My phone rang and I excused myself to take the call. I walked over by the back door. "Hello?"

"I'm looking for Kim Murphy, the private investigator."

"That's me," I said.

"My name is Carl Tipton. I heard you wanted to speak to me about Derek."

"Yes. Uh, when would be a good time for you?" I asked.

"Never. Don't contact me or my wife again. If you do, I'll have you arrested for harassment." There was silence for a moment and then a dial tone.

"Asshole," I muttered. I turned to go back to the table and froze. In the partially open drawer in the china hutch were several large nails. The kind used on roofs.

"Miss Murphy, you'll have to excuse me. I'm tired. I need to rest."

I tore my eyes from the nails and plastered on a smile. I tried to ignore the pounding in my ears. "Sure. No problem." Barbara walked me to the front door. I stepped outside and turned back around. "Miss Greer, have you had any work done on your home? A new roof or a remodeling job perhaps?" I asked.

"Of course not. What kind of question is that?"

Her eyes got big. "You don't think I killed Derek?" she asked.

"Oops, gotta go," I said, and walked as fast as my legs would go back to my car. Once inside, I locked the doors and sped off. A few streets away, I pulled over and called Grant. I left a message asking him to call me back. I calmly explained to the voice mail that it was urgent.

Instead of going back to the office, I decided to head home and wait for Grant's call. I only hoped Barbara wasn't disposing of evidence in the meantime. After several hours of attempting to distract myself, first with a book, then with TV, and finally with food, I tried Grant's cell phone. Once again it went straight to voice mail. I was getting so frustrated I was about to scream. Just when I thought he would never return my call, my cell phone rang. I glanced down at the display and screamed.

"It's about time. What took you so long?" I asked.

"I'm on a stakeout. What's so important?"

"Oh nothing, just that I may have solved the Derek Patterson murder."

Grant sighed. "Kim…"

"Where are you?" I asked.

I must have startled him because he actually told me.

"Great. I can be there in five."

"Kim, you can't—"

I hung up the phone before he could finish his warning about showing up while he was working but this was important. I had to clear Aunt Tessa's name. I took off and drove across town. I spotted his car parked across from the low income housing apartments. I parked behind his car and knocked on the window. The door locks clicked and I opened the door and slid into the passenger's seat.

"What are you doing here?" Grant asked.

"Looking for you," I replied.

"Good. You've found me. Now go home."

"You have to listen to me. I think Derek's pregnant girlfriend may have killed him. At first I wondered if it was the first girlfriend but I don't think so."

"Kim, what the hell are you talking about?"

"Derek Patterson's murder, hello?"

Grant shifted in his seat. Tearing his gaze from the apartments, he turned and stared directly into my eyes. "What girlfriends?" he asked.

"Well, there's his partner's wife, Mrs. Tipton, but I don't think she did it because while she was busy doing Derek, Derek's wife was doing Mr. Tipton."

"Have you been drinking?"

"No, but that sounds like a good idea. Are you buying?" I asked.

"Okay, I think I got this, but then who is the second girlfriend, the pregnant one?" he asked.

"Oh good, you were paying attention." I smiled. Grant frowned. "Okay, okay. She's the redhead who lives in the same neighborhood as the Pattersons and Aunt Tessa. She said Derek told her he was going to leave his wife for her and the baby but I don't think so." I stopped to take a breath. "I think that when Barbara told Derek she was pregnant, he flipped out. She got angry and bang."

"And bang Derek's dead?"

"Exactly."

"Okay, so where's your proof?"

"The roofing nails," I said.

Grant's eyes narrowed. "What roofing nails?"

"The ones I found in Barbara's kitchen," I said.

"Wait a minute, that's it? No nail gun, no bloody clothes, just nails?"

"Yeah, so?"

"So, after that storm last month, half the buildings in town have roofing nails."

"Okay, but she said she didn't have any work done. Plus, why would they be in her kitchen?" I asked.

"Because she found them on the ground and put them there for safekeeping."

I opened my mouth to speak but Grant raised his hand. "That's what even a third rate attorney will tell the judge."

I knew he was right but I didn't care. I just wanted this case over. "Aunt Tessa didn't kill him."

"I want you to be right. I'm starting to think I was a bit hasty in arresting her."

I smiled. I knew that had to be hard for him to admit. I didn't pester him with questions. They could wait, for now. "Thanks for that," I said.

He nodded and glanced out his window. "Oh shit." He started the car and put it in gear; he checked both ways before pulling into traffic. "Look, as soon as you can, I'm going to have you get out. I'll call one of the patrol officers and they can give you a ride back to your car."

"No way, this is fun. Who are you following? What did they do?" I asked while buckling my seatbelt.

"I'm not telling you that. Just sit there and be quiet."

"Fine," I muttered.

We followed the person around town, first heading north then west before heading south. Eventually, the silver Mercedes pulled into a driveway of a duplex. A short man, five feet eight at most, balding head, and the beginnings of a beer belly got out of the car and walked up to the front door.

Grant drove on past and turned into a driveway. He turned toward me. "Okay, out you go."

"I don't think so."

"Kim, you can't stay in the car. I'm working."

"I know, but there is no way you're letting me out here."

Grant looked around. "What is wrong with here?" he asked.

"Nothing, except my sister's nosy friend, Olivia, lives two houses down. If she sees me, she'll come outside and want to talk. She's also on the neighborhood watch. How long do you think it'll take for it to get back to Mr. Mercedes he's being watched by the cops?" I asked.

Grant muttered something about people keeping their mouths shut. He parked several houses down with a clear view of the front of the building. He cracked the windows and shut the car off.

"Oh my God. Are you nuts? We'll die without air conditioning," I said.

"I'm fine, but you're more than welcome to leave."

"No chance. If you can handle it, so can I." I smiled.

"Uh-huh."

"I can. I'll bet you twenty bucks I last longer than you do."

"Kim, gambling is illegal."

"That isn't gambling."

"It is according to the law."

"So, arrest me. Lock me up and put me in a cell." I put my hands out in front of me, wrists touching.

Grant's eyes locked onto my arms. He leaned over and gently pulled my left arm to his lips. "There are dozens of things I'd love to do to you, but locking you up isn't one of them."

He stared into my eyes as his lips brushed against my skin. I gasped as my nipples tightened. My southern region instantly joined the party, making its need apparent. I tried to pull my arm away but Grant's grip tightened. "Grant, stop. We can't. Not here."

"I could change your mind." His voice was huskier than the teasing tone just a moment before.

"Oh, I want to, but I just don't want to be on the evening news. I'm pretty sure my family would kill us both."

Grant shook his head. "Right." He released my

arm after placing a kiss on the inside of my wrist and elbow.

I groaned. "You don't play fair."

He laughed. "Sorry, sweetheart. Afraid our vociferous lovemaking would disturb the homeowners here."

"Wow. Look who owns a dictionary." I turned to the side and leaned against the car door.

"Ha-ha."

"So, what are we going to do while we wait?" I asked. Grant looked at me and smirked. "I didn't mean that."

"We could try being quiet," he said, focusing his attention back to the car.

"We could talk."

"I don't think so. That gets us into too much trouble," Grant said.

"Fine."

"Fine.

Over the next twenty minutes we sat in silence as the inside of the car quickly reached oven-like temperatures. I was giving this thing five more minutes and then I was calling Charmaine for a ride home. Luckily the driver of the Mercedes came out of the house and got into his car. A minute later, he pulled out of the driveway and drove toward us.

Grant turned to the side and pulled me against him. Sadly, the kiss was over all too soon. Grant quickly started the car and turned around. We caught up to the Mercedes at the end of the block. After a few minutes, he pulled into a convenience store parking lot. Grant parked in the laundromat lot with a perfect view of the car.

As we waited for the driver to return the sun dropped lower and lower in the sky. If only it had taken the warm temperatures with it. A woman walked out of the convenience store with a bottle of wine in each hand. I looked at Grant and smirked. "I guess it's just a two bottle kind of night."

"I know the feeling."

"Me too."

"I'm calling this a night. How about if I buy us a bottle of wine? Hell, I'll even add in some Italian takeout and some Reese's minis for later."

"Sounds great, but what about Mr. Mercedes?" I asked.

"He'll come out in a few minutes with a carton of cigarettes, some beer, and snack foods before heading back to your sister's friend's neighbor's house where he'll stay until morning. At least that's been his pattern for the last month."

"Good. Let's go. I'm starving."

Grant pulled out of the parking lot. As we drove past, the driver walked outside and headed straight for his car. Grant dropped me off at mine and agreed to meet me at my place soon. I drove home and let myself in through the back door. I avoided looking at the apartment next to mine. The last thing I needed was one more embarrassing encounter with my new neighbors.

I headed straight to the kitchen and poured myself a glass of ice water. After the free car sauna I was dangerously dehydrated. I sat at the counter and considered taking a quick shower but I didn't think I had time. I knew Grant was going to get food but if he went to the place he usually went there was never a long wait on carry-out orders. It had been that way for as long as I could remember.

I passed on the shower as an idea began to take root. I dug a cooler out of one of the cabinets and filled it with ice cubes. When I thought it had plenty I stuffed ten bottled waters inside. On top of those I put two Hershey's Bars I'd rescued from the bottom of my purse.

In the living room I took two blankets and a couple of pillows. I was all set when someone knocked on the back door. I opened the door and found Grant standing there, arms filled with brown bags.

"Let me in."

"I had an idea."

"I don't think I can survive too many more of your ideas," Grant said.

"You really are quite the comedian, aren't you?"

"I try. What's up?"

"Since I helped you with your stakeout, I thought it would be good if you helped me with one."

"What about the food and the wine?" He lifted the bags higher to show me. "Wait a minute, you didn't help me. You invited yourself and insisted—"

"We leave the wine here for later. The rest comes with us and we have a picnic in the car. I even got us pillows, blankets, and a cooler with bottled water and chocolate."

"Wow, how could a guy pass that up? Have any bug spray?"

"No."

He sighed. "Let's go before I change my mind."

"Awesome. I promise you won't regret this," I said.

"Too late for that."

After sticking both bottles of wine in the refrigerator, we loaded his car because he refused to be a passenger in mine—what a guy thing—and he followed my directions to Barbara's house. He parked across the street, away from the glare of the streetlight.

"So, what exactly do you hope to learn by sitting here watching her house?"

"I don't know. Maybe she'll incriminate herself."

"You know that only happens on TV or in movies, right?"

"It could happen. She could panic and decide to dispose of evidence, like bloody clothes or the murder weapon."

"Sure, and the Dallas Cowboys could call tomorrow and sign me up as their star quarterback."

"Dallas? Really? I'd think you more a Jets fan."

"The team doesn't matter because it isn't going to happen, and neither is this woman doing something illegal in her front yard."

"Whatever, let's eat."

I dug into the cooler and put bottles of water in our cup holders while Grant dug into the bags. Much to my delight the container he handed me was filled with chicken Alfredo and fettuccini. Grant opened another container that had breadsticks.

"You are amazing," I told him.

"I know."

189

We devoured our food while watching, and in my case, praying, for Barbara to do something suspicious. When we were done, I packed the containers back into the now empty bags. We sat and talked about nothing of importance for a couple of hours. Eventually Grant had enough.

"Okay, if we leave now, we can make it to Dairy Queen before it closes. Why don't we split a brownie sundae?" Grant asked.

I looked over to see if he was serious or joking. He seemed serious, so I had to set him straight. "Grant, that's sweet, but dessert is the best part of the meal. It's even more important than the potatoes or the pasta."

He laughed. "Okay, I'll order two."

"Smart man."

With one last look at Barbara's house we sped off. We arrived at the drive-thru just in time. We parked in the lot and ate our dessert. Grant finished first. He leaned over and wiped the corner of my mouth then licked his finger. I groaned.

"Oh, sorry, you had chocolate on your lip."

"Let's go back to my place. Now."

CHAPTER TEN

I was being smothered by a giant cloud. I opened my eyes and found myself cocooned in my comforter. I unwrapped myself and gasped for fresh air. I reached for the other side of the bed before remembering that Grant had already left.

When we'd gotten home last night, we'd come directly upstairs. Eventually we'd made our way back downstairs and shared a bottle of wine before racing upstairs to the bedroom. I glanced at the clock. Grant had gotten a call and rushed out before the sun had dared to show up. He kissed me goodbye and I had mumbled something I thought sounded like bye before rolling over and going back to sleep.

I dragged myself out of bed and into the bathroom. Since I decided to skip the gym, I hopped in the shower. After I got out, I blow-dried my hair, put it up in a ponytail, and got dressed in a pair of black jeans and a gray short-sleeved blouse. I took a few minutes to apply mascara and lipstick before heading downstairs in a desperate search for

191

caffeine and breakfast.

I started a pot of coffee then searched the pantry and refrigerator. I settled on scrambled eggs, toast, and several strips of bacon. When it was ready, I took my breakfast into the living room and ate in front of the morning news.

I managed to watch for a whole ten minutes before I felt like throwing the remote control. I wasn't sure but that might have been a new record. I turned off the TV and finished eating. I cleaned up the kitchen and the dishes. Then, when I couldn't stall any longer, I left for the office.

I arrived to find Mrs. Patterson waiting for me in the parking lot. I had been hoping to put it off but I guessed now was as good a time as any to tell her what I knew, minus the baby news, and to move on. I had a killer to find and I was running out of ideas. Actually, I'd run out a few days ago, but whatever.

Mrs. Patterson followed me inside. I had her take a seat while I made a fresh pot of coffee. A few minutes later, I walked into my office with two mugs. I handed one to her before sitting down in my seat with my own.

"I'm sorry. I just couldn't wait. Did you talk to her? What did she say?" Mrs. Patterson lifted the cup to her mouth and sipped.

"I didn't learn much. She just wants to move on with her life. Which I think is the best thing for everyone," I said.

"Yes, of course, it's just so hard. I just keep going through my house wondering what she's touched. Looking at my bed and thinking, how many times did they have sex in my bed?" Her blonde hair was in a single braid. She reached up and began to fiddle with it.

"You don't need to worry about that. She was never at your house," I lied.

"Oh, thank goodness." Mrs. Patterson sighed. "I feel much better. I was afraid I was going to have to get rid of everything or move."

"Well, now you don't have to. You should be able to go home, relax, and start the healing process," I said.

"Thank you. That would be great."

"Glad I could help."

Mrs. Patterson put her cup down on the desk. "Have you heard anything else about my husband's case?" she asked.

"No, nothing."

"Do you think maybe she had something to do with Derek's murder?"

"I, uh, don't think so, but I promise if I hear anything, I'll let you know."

"Good. I'm having a hard time sleeping. I can't get used to the idea there's a killer out there waiting to get caught. I close my eyes at night, terrified the person will come back and get me."

I tried reassuring her everything would be fine but honestly I had no idea if it would be or not. I didn't know who killed her husband or why. All I could assume was that the person responsible would want to keep his or her distance from the widow. At least I sincerely hoped so for her sake. After we finished our coffee, I showed Mrs. Patterson to the front door. She shook my hand and thanked me for all the hard work I was doing and for my discretion.

"Between his family and the nosy reporters I just can't take anything else right now," Mrs. Patterson said.

"I'm sure it's been awful. It will get better. It just takes time."

She smiled, thanked me, and walked to her car. I closed the door and was walking toward my office when I heard my cell phone ring. I ran down the hall and into my office.

"Hello," I said.

"Where are you?" Grant asked.

"My office. Why?"

"Stay there. I'm on my way," he said before hanging up.

That was odd, even for Grant. I couldn't tell if he was angry, frustrated, or just annoyed. I guessed it didn't matter because I'd find out soon enough. I just hoped whatever it was wasn't directed at me. I sat at my desk and wondered if there was anything I'd done in the last couple of days that could have set him off. Nothing came to mind, but unfortunately that didn't put my mind at ease.

It turned out I didn't have long to wait and worry. Grant showed up while I was getting myself another cup of coffee. I took one look at him and filled up another mug and handed it to him.

"Thanks," Grant said.

"No problem. What's up?" I asked.

"Tell me you didn't make an anonymous call to the station about a certain redhead."

"Huh?"

"Did you call and report Miss Greer for digging a hole in her backyard?"

"What the hell are you talking about?"

"This morning, Barbara Greer was arrested for murder."

"What? Son of a bitch. No way. What happened?" I asked.

"We got a call about Miss Greer's suspicious activity. I showed up, didn't even have a warrant, but she let me in. Nothing was amiss until I looked out the window. There was a freshly dug hole in her backyard. Guess what we found inside," Grant said.

"Oh my God, the nail gun!" I shouted.

"Yup. You were right," he said. He took another sip of coffee. "The DA is formally dropping charges against Mrs. Boudreaux."

"That's great."

"I thought you'd be a bit happier about the news," he said.

"I am. I'm just surprised, that's all."

"Don't be. You were right." He emptied his mug. "I've gotta get back. I just wanted to tell you in person," Grant said.

"Thanks. Oh, I've got to call Charmaine and Shandra."

"They'll probably want to thank you."

"For what?"

"Fine, don't admit it, but thanks for helping." He kissed me on the cheek and turned to leave.

"But I didn't do anything," I said.

"Don't worry, your secret is safe with me."

After Grant left I sat back down at my desk, glad the killer was caught and Aunt Tessa would be free. My phone rang, disrupting my thoughts. "Hello."

"Kim, get your butt over here," Charmaine

shouted into my ear.

"You've heard?"

"Hell yeah. Thank goodness. This mess was giving me nightmares."

"I bet."

"So, get over here. Aunt Tessa wants to thank you. We all do. Later we're having a party to celebrate."

"That's great but I didn't—"

"Good. We'll see you in a few." And with that, Charmaine hung up.

I didn't rush right over. I was thrilled for Aunt Tessa and her whole family. I knew she was innocent but I just had an odd feeling. Whatever it was I had to get over it. I shut the coffeemaker off and washed the mugs before locking up and driving over to Aunt Tessa's house.

I was met with hugs and shouts of joy. The house was already half-filled with family and friends. Charmaine and Shandra were running around. Aunt Tessa asked to speak to me privately. I followed her through the house and into the backyard.

"Kim, I just wanted to thank you for what you did," Aunt Tessa said.

"Aunt Tessa, I didn't do anything," I protested.

"Oh, young lady, don't lie to me. I've already talked to that detective of yours, and I don't believe that story for a second."

"I really—"

"Look, you were there for me and for those precious girls in there. I can't thank you enough for that."

"That's what you do for the people you love."

"That's right. Charmaine said you didn't doubt me for a second."

"Of course not. Anyone who knows you wouldn't believe you killed someone," I said.

"You know that's the truth. If I had, I certainly wouldn't have left him in my rose bushes." She laughed.

"Exactly. I know how hard you've worked on those." I smiled.

Aunt Tessa hugged me and told me she was tired and was going to go upstairs and rest for a bit. She promised to come back down later. After several attempts to leave failed, I finally gave up. Melissa showed up with several bottles of champagne to add to the party mood.

I spent the rest of the afternoon being hugged, thanked, and offered tons of food, most of which I kindly declined. Eventually, Aunt Tessa returned and the party began in earnest. I had managed to relax and was actually having fun when I looked up and spotted Zack walking down the hall.

I sucked in a breath. I looked away, wishing I could make myself disappear. Since that wasn't going to happen, and I didn't have an invisibility cloak or a transporter from *Star Trek*, all I could do was pretend to be interested in bees. Charmaine's great-uncle James was a beekeeper. He was going on and on about all the wonderful products that could be made from honey. All I could think of was why so many people enjoyed bee spit on their biscuits.

That and how hot Zack looked in his dark suit

and tie. Then again he looked even better completely naked. This was so not the time to be thinking about Zack naked or otherwise. This was about Aunt Tessa.

I stuffed myself with food and managed to keep several steps away from Zack. Finally, exhausted and drained, I pulled Charmaine and Shandra aside and told them I was heading home. After several protests I was able to escape. I had just opened my car door when a hand touched my shoulder, I spun around prepared to knock some jerk on his ass and found myself face to face with Zack.

He lifted his hands and backed up a few steps. "Relax, it's just me," Zack said.

"How was I supposed to know that?" I asked.

"Maybe because you spent the last few hours avoiding me?"

"I wasn't avoiding you. I was busy."

"Uh-huh," he said.

"Would you put your hands down? You look like an idiot."

He put his hands down and slid them into his front pockets. Watching this had thoughts going on around my head I had no business thinking. I shook my head, hoping to clear out the cobwebs. "I've gotta go. See ya."

"Before you go, I just wanted to tell you nice job."

"I didn't…whatever. Bye."

"Bye. Drive safe," Zack said.

"I always do."

He turned and walked back up the driveway. In the quiet I could clearly hear his laughter trail behind him.

Back home, I locked up behind me and dragged myself up the stairs to my bedroom. I stripped out of my clothes and into a set of Eeyore pajamas. I spent a few minutes in the bathroom brushing my teeth and scrubbing my face. Back in my room, I crawled under the covers. I grabbed a book from the bedside table and began to read.

I opened my eyes and frowned. My eyes hurt. I hadn't gotten out of bed yet and I was already exhausted. I guessed I was getting too old to stay up all night reading and expect to be in tiptop shape in the morning. That sucked but it was so worth it. I'd always choose sleep deprivation to read a good book.

After a few minutes of stalling, I got out of bed and went about my morning routine of getting ready. Only this time I skipped making breakfast and went to the nearest McDonald's drive-thru for a large coffee, two hash browns, and an order of hotcakes, which every place else just called pancakes.

I sat at my desk and ate my breakfast and drank my coffee while searching the web. I checked one of our local news station's sites for the arrest. I clicked on the link and began to read. Ms. Greer was being held without bail. She was charged with the murder of Derek Patterson.

Somehow the reporters had managed to get a picture of Barbara being led away in handcuffs. I kind of felt sorry for her. In a matter of months she would be going to jail and her innocent baby would be put into the system. Hopefully Barbara had family or friends who could raise the baby and avoid the nightmarish foster system. I figured it was kind of hard to find a family willing to take a kid whose mom had killed the dad. Yikes.

I finished the story and clicked on another when I heard banging on the front door. In my eagerness to eat breakfast I had forgotten to unlock the door. I looked at my food and frowned. Maybe I should ignore it, or I could make whoever it was go away. That would be nice. Unless of course they were paying customers. Now that was someone I didn't want to chase away.

I opened the door and plastered on a fake smile I sincerely hoped looked real. When I saw who was standing on my doorstep the smile collapsed.

"Mrs. Patterson, what are you doing here?" I asked, though I was pretty damned sure I knew what she wanted.

She walked past me. "Did you know?" she asked.

"Excuse me?"

"Did you know that slut killed my husband?"

I knew this would take a while. I closed the door and walked back to my office, Mrs. Patterson hot on my heels. I sat in my chair and motioned for her to have a seat. "No, I didn't know," I replied. Which was the truth, sort of.

"But why? Why would she kill him?" Mrs. Patterson asked.

"I don't know." I did have a sneaking suspicion but I didn't want to drag that out in the open. Surely that ugly business would be front page news before, during, and after the trial. The public would know far too many personal details about everyone involved. Yet another reason I hated reporters.

"I'm so confused."

"I'm sure you are. Why don't you go home, get into your favorite pajamas, and try to get some rest. You probably haven't slept in days," I said.

"I haven't. Whenever I try to sleep I toss and turn for hours. If I do fall asleep, I have the most horrible nightmares. Then I wake up and realize I'm living a nightmare."

"I'm so sorry for what you're going through," I said.

"Thank you. Thank you for everything." She stood up. "I'm going to take your advice. Get some rest and move on with my life."

"Good idea."

"It is pathetic really. I've been at home crying my eyes out over the man who was screwing around on me."

"You loved him and he's gone. The rest will fade away in time."

"Exactly. Plus, he left me set for life, so whatever else he was, I'm provided for."

"That's nice," I said around a sudden lump in my throat. I had a feeling if Barbara was telling the truth about Derek being her baby's father, some of that money may end up going to the baby. Since that was the last thing Mrs. Patterson needed to hear, I let it drop. I smiled and shook her hand. "Good luck."

"Thanks." She turned and left my office.

I let out a sigh of relief when I heard the outer door close. I tossed my now cold breakfast in the trash. With Aunt Tessa's case closed it was time I got back to making a living. I had bills to pay. I dug Mr. Larson's business card out of my wallet. I sat and stared at it for quite a while. When I'd finally run out of excuses, I picked up my phone and dialed. I was preparing to leave a message when Mr. Larson answered on the fourth ring.

"Larson speaking."

"Hello, Mr. Larson, this is Kim Murphy."

"Miss Murphy, what a pleasure to hear your voice. To what do I owe the pleasure?" Mr. Larson asked.

"I, um, was thinking about your case."

"Wonderful. If you're free tonight, I can send my car for you."

Well, crap, the last thing I needed was to be in his house at night. I could think of far less dangerous places to be, like, say, the fast lane on the freeway.

"Sorry, I have plans. What about my office this afternoon?"

"I'm afraid I have a couple of meetings."

I thought for a second. "Okay, I can rearrange some things but we'll need to meet somewhere less out of the way," I said.

"Fine. I know just the place." He gave me an address that was only a block or so away from the police station. I agreed to meet him there at seven and hung up. I turned on my computer and googled the address.

I groaned at the screen. I couldn't believe I'd just agreed to meet a possible killer at the most expensive and exclusive restaurant in a forty-mile radius. It took months to get a reservation, or so I'd heard. Supposedly none of the menus had prices. They figured if you couldn't afford it, your reservation wouldn't have been approved. Yikes. I couldn't imagine eating at a place where you needed an excellent credit rating and a six-figure income just to get in the door.

Now, I had another problem. I wasn't sure what to wear. What was appropriate attire for a dinner meeting at a fancy-shmancy restaurant? More importantly, a dinner meeting with a client arrested for murder.

I spent the rest of the afternoon googling Mr. Nathan Larson and reading numerous articles about him. I almost called and cancelled the meeting. Then I remembered the balance in my checking account. Deciding to call it a day, I shut down my computer, locked up the office, and drove home.

I stared at my closet. Nothing jumped out at me shouting, "*Pick me. Pick me.*" I didn't own anything with a fancy designer label. I did have several nice dresses I'd worn to church, holidays, and Sunday dinners with my family. After debating my limited options, I decided to go with a little black dress. That should do me well, no matter what the situation.

With that done, I went downstairs in search of food. If TV shows were to be believed, the fancier, more expensive the restaurant, the smaller the food portions. This made absolutely no sense whatsoever. I could spend twenty bucks at the local Chinese place and end up with enough food to feed six people and have enough leftovers for lunch the next day.

Whatever. What did I know? At least I wasn't going to be paying for tonight's exquisite cuisine. I didn't live on sprouts and vegetables. I had an average appetite and the last thing I wanted was to be embarrassed by my stomach growling halfway through the meal. I settled on half of a turkey sandwich, a handful of Mike-Sells potato chips, and a can of Diet Coke. I took my pre-dinner into the living room and sat on the couch. I flipped on the TV for noise and read Kate Collins's latest cozy mystery.

I was just about to find out who the killer was when my phone rang. I was tempted to ignore it. I hated being interrupted when I was reading but my curiosity won out, as it usually did. "Hello."

"Oh, thank goodness, Miss Murphy. It's Barbara, Barbara Greer. Please don't hang up."

I hadn't been going to, which made me wonder just how many people she called already and had done just that.

"What can I do for you?" I asked, confused as to why she was calling me. She must be extremely desperate.

"I need your help."

Just as I'd thought. The poor girl must have no one else. "Miss Greer, I'm not sure how I could help you," I said.

"I want to hire you. I've been set up and these cops don't care. Please."

"Miss Greer, I don't think that's such a good idea…"

"I can pay you. My dad is wealthy and I'm pretty

sure he wouldn't let his first grandchild be born in prison," Barbara said.

My hesitation wasn't about the money, it was about Aunt Tessa. I was pretty sure she'd been set up, and despite my own involvement in getting Barbara arrested, I still hadn't felt sure she was guilty. Though, when I'd snuck out and gone back to her place, I'd been shocked to see her carrying a box from the garage to the backyard. When I'd walked over to the fence and seen her with her back to me, burying something in the yard, I'd done what I'd had to do. Not that I'd ever let anyone know it had been me. That was one secret I was most assuredly taking to the grave with me. Right along with my weight and the number of men I'd been with. The number was low enough I could count on one hand and not have a finger left, but still, that was my business and no one else's.

"Hello?"

"Sorry, I'm still here. I just think maybe you should hire someone else."

"No. I feel comfortable with you. I trust you. Please. Help me, Miss Murphy."

On a hunch I asked her the question that had been bugging me ever since I'd made the call. "Where did you get the nail gun?"

"I never had a nail gun. It wasn't me. I swear."

She gave me her father's name and phone number as well as the contact information for her attorney. I agreed to think about it and let her know. I hung up with mixed emotions. I felt like I was betraying Aunt Tessa, Charmaine, and Shandra. I knew that was silly but I couldn't help it.

Feeling grimy from even taking the call, I decided to take a second shower for the day. In my rush to get ready, I glanced at the clock and realized I had finished with twenty minutes to spare. Grateful for the unexpected reading time, I finished the book.

I put the book down and went in search of my purse when the doorbell rang. I changed directions and headed for the door. I opened it and found Grant looking as hot as always standing on my front porch—all four feet of it.

Grant's eyes did a slow up and down and repeated the process. He smiled. "Nice."

"Thanks," I said, willing myself to ignore the spike in my blood pressure and the rasp in my voice caused by his perusal of me.

"I was going to see if you wanted to hang out but I guess you already have plans." Grant frowned.

"I'm working."

"Dressed like that?" he asked.

"I'm meeting a client for dinner."

"Must be some client."

"I'd say annoying and stubborn would sum him up."

"So, who is this client you are all dressed up for?"

"Grant, you know I'm not going to answer that. But, I'm free tomorrow night if you'd like to do something. How about pizza and a six-pack?" I asked.

"Sounds good." He pulled me against him then leaned down. Our lips met. I was suddenly extremely hungry, but not for food. Grant's hand slid down my back and rested on my hip.

The sound of someone clearing their throat had Grant and I jumping apart like a pair of teenagers caught making out on the front porch. I glanced over and groaned. My client, Mr. Larson, dressed in a black tuxedo, stood a few feet away, smiling.

"I'm so sorry to have intruded, but you did say seven o'clock," Mr. Larson said.

Grant looked at Mr. Larson and his eyes narrowed while his face flushed. I'd have bet his was not from embarrassment, like mine, but from anger.

"Excuse us for a moment." Grant grasped my hand and practically dragged me behind him into my apartment, his behavior confirming my suspicion. Once inside, he let go of my hand and spun around.

"Are you insane? Do you have any idea who that is?"

"I would appreciate it if you wouldn't question my mental health at the top of your lungs. Of course I know who he is," I said, taking several steps away from the entryway. "He's my client."

Grant sucked in a breath. I immediately wished I could retract my words. "You are *not* going anywhere with him."

I chose to ignore his ordering me around, for now. "I have to. I already agreed to go."

"Then tell him you've come to your senses and changed your mind."

I rolled my eyes. "That would be rude."

Grant slammed his right fist into his left hand. "You're worried about being rude to a murder suspect?"

I thought for a moment. "Actually, yeah."

Grant smirked. "Finally, you're making sense."

"Ha-ha-ha."

"Look, I'm worried about you."

I would think about the warm fuzzy feelings that statement gave me later. Right now I had to convince the modern day caveman I was capable of taking care of myself. "It's just dinner. We'll be in a public place, and I'll have my cell phone."

"What about the limo waiting out front?" Grant asked.

"Uh…"

Grant spun around, yanked the door open, and marched outside. I raced after him, hoping to prevent him from doing something stupid. I arrived in time to see Grant waving his badge in front of Mr. Larson's face.

"Let me make something clear to you. Nothing happens to her," Grant said, pointing at me. "If she so much as gets a scratch, there won't be enough left of you to bury, much less prosecute."

Mr. Larson smiled and raised his hands. "I understand, detective. Rest assured, Miss Murphy is in no danger."

Grant glared at Mr. Larson before turning toward me. "Call me when you get to the restaurant, when you leave the restaurant, and when you get home."

"Jeez, why don't you just put a tracking system on me?" I muttered.

"Don't tempt me."

I raised my hand. "I promise to call you."

Grant frowned.

"I'll even call you when I go to the bathroom." I smiled.

Grant muttered something that sounded a lot like *smart-ass* before throwing one last look at Mr. Larson and stomping off.

"Sorry about that," I said.

"That's quite all right. I understand his concerns."

I followed Mr. Larson to the waiting limousine and had a moment of panic. I hated to think that all of Grant's dire warnings of doom were affecting me but maybe he had a point. I took a deep breath and slowly let it out before stepping inside the limo. Since I assumed Mr. Larson would sit facing forward, I chose the backward facing seat. My guess had been correct when he took a seat across from me. He smiled, and once the door was closed, offered me a drink, which I politely declined, choosing to keep a clear head. He helped himself to something amber colored.

I tried to sit back, relax, and enjoy the ride, but that was impossible thanks to Grant's words repeatedly floating around in my head like an annoying song stuck on repeat. I was positive that had been his intention all along.

Mr. Larson spent the next fifteen minutes attempting to regale me with both the number of and unusual qualities of the locations he'd traveled to recently. I smiled and pretended to be interested but I personally was a homebody. Even if my bank account had been brimming with a one followed by six or seven zeros, I would prefer to hang out at home. Though I could see myself temporarily giving up the couch potato routine for a quick trip to Italy, Ireland, and France. There was no way I'd go to the Australian Outback—didn't he realize just how many deadly snakes they had there? No freaking way.

The car stopped and I slid my hand into my purse, sighing in relief as my hand closed around my Glock 9mm, the best protection eight hundred bucks could buy. Plus, thanks to regular visits to the shooting range, I could hit a hell of a lot more than the broad side of a barn, unless my target was moving quickly from side to side, then I'd have a bit of trouble.

Mr. Larson stepped out of the car first and reached for my hand. I held on long enough to exit the vehicle before removing my hand from his. We walked side by side toward a front door tall enough to let an eight-foot man walk through upright without needing to bend down.

Once inside, I looked around and was surprised at the normalcy of the place. I wasn't sure what I'd been expecting, but for the amount of money the place charged, a little gold leaf here and a crystal chandelier there wouldn't be out of place, but then what did I know about interior design.

Black, gray, and cream covered everything from the walls to the carpet to the tablecloths. A clean-shaven gentleman with dark hair and eyes in a black suit and bow tie escorted us to our table. He held out the chair for me. I smiled my thanks and his attention turned toward my dining companion.

"Mr. Larson, what a pleasure to see you again."

"Thanks, Davis. How's the family?"

"They're doing wonderfully. Thank you for asking."

"Davis, please bring me a bottle from my personal collection," Mr. Larson said.

"Of course, right away." He bowed toward us before rushing off.

Mr. Larson had just finished explaining how the restaurant kept a supply of his favorite wine on hand for whenever he dined there. Once the wine arrived at the table he went on and on and on, much to my despair, about all of its amazing qualities. I assumed that just meant it was extremely expensive.

He swirled a small amount of wine in his glass. He also held it up to the light and sniffed it before taking a sip. I sure hoped he didn't expect me to do any of that because yikes, I'd likely end up wearing half of it.

My phone rang and I realized I'd forgotten to text Grant when we arrived. I pulled the phone out of my purse, expecting to see a terse message from Grant. Instead there was a frantic text from Mrs. Patterson. I excused myself from the table and went in search of the nearest ladies' room. After a brief search, I found it. A set of double doors opened into a vaulted ceiling entrance with a crystal chandelier large enough to compete with the ball dropped in Times Square each New Year's Eve.

The first thing I did after closing my gaping mouth was to text Grant and inform him I'd arrived safely at the restaurant. Next, I replied to Mrs. Patterson's text, explaining to her I was currently busy but I would call her as soon as I was available.

I returned to the table to find a waiter placing

several large dishes piled high with food all around Mr. Larson's place and mine. It was odd as we hadn't ordered anything. It turned out the menu each night was set and no one ever did anything as pedestrian as *order* their meals. Odd. That would be the best way for me to describe the very rich.

Earlier I had done my best to avoid panicking over the multiple pieces of silverware. I hadn't been raised in a barn, but I could never remember if you started nearest the plate or furthest away from the plate. I didn't see what all the fuss what about. As long as you weren't picking it up with your hands or chewing with your mouth open, who cared.

"Is everything all right?" Mr. Larson asked.

"Yes. I just had to calm someone down."

He frowned. "Your boyfriend seemed quite upset when we left." He lifted his glass. "You hadn't told him about our dinner plans."

"Grant is not my boyfriend, he's…" I didn't finish the sentence because I wasn't quite sure just exactly what Grant and I were. "He's someone I care about, but he tends to be a bit over-protective at times."

"Excellent." Mr. Larson took a sip from his glass and set it down.

"Huh?"

"When a man is interested in a woman he wants to scope out any possible competition." He smiled and picked up a fork.

"Mr. Larson, we have a business relationship. Nothing personal is going to happen," I said.

"Of course not. Not now anyway. Right now, I will need all of your attention focused on my upcoming trial."

"Fine. Just so there's no misunderstanding."

Mr. Larson smiled. "I understand perfectly. You might want to warn your friend we'll have to be spending quite a lot of time together. I hope he enjoys dining alone."

After two of the longest hours of my life, I was safely dropped off back at my place, after politely declining an offer of a nightcap. I had just closed the door when someone began knocking on it. I peeked out the peephole and sighed. I plastered on a fake smile and opened the door.

"Grant, what a lovely surprise."

"You didn't call," he said.

"I texted you twice from the restaurant. What else did you want me to do? Take you with me."

"You shouldn't have gone at all," he snapped.

"Look, I don't want to fight. I want to get out of these clothes and call it a night."

Grant's eyes started at my feet, stuffed into two-inch black heels, and worked their way up my body, stopping not so briefly at my chest before finally settling on my face. "I could help you with that." He smiled.

My body started to tingle in all the right places. "I think that's a great idea. These zippers can be a pain." I turned slightly to reveal the back of the dress.

Grant's eyes narrowed. He reached over and pulled me against him. I felt the bulge in his pants and groaned. His lips locked onto mine as his hands grabbed onto the zipper. I tore my lips from his and took a step back. "Upstairs," I whispered. Before I

213

could move, I gasped as the heat of his skin sent shock waves up and down my spine. Suddenly I was standing before him in a matching bra and panties set from the amazing Victoria's Secret catalog, the dress pooled around my feet.

Grant picked me up and carried me to the couch. He sat down with me on his lap. Grant's rough hands wouldn't stay in one place. One moment they were cupping my butt the next they were rubbing against my breasts.

"Oh God, I've thought about this all day," he said against my lips.

"Me too." I arched my back, giving him full access to my chest.

CHAPTER ELEVEN

A buzzing sound woke me from a wonderful dream I was having. It involved chocolate cake, ice cream, and a deliciously yummy six-pack—of abs. After several attempts I finally pried my eyes open and found Grant looking down at me.

"Good, you're awake. I have to go."

Remembering my dream, I reached up, grabbed his tie, and pulled his lips to mine. After a few minutes, we both came up for air. "Don't go," I said.

"Kim, I'd love to stay in bed with you all day but I've got a dead body waiting for me."

"Well, it isn't going anywhere. Maybe it could wait. Just a few minutes." I smiled.

"You know I can't just let…" Grant sucked in a breath. "Holy Hell. You are a very bad influence, Miss Murphy."

While he was talking I'd tossed the blanket aside, revealing my naked body. "What should we do about that, detective?"

"I don't know about you, but I'm gonna thank

215

my lucky stars."

Grant eventually left for his crime scene. I walked into the bathroom and noticed the smile on my face that didn't seem interested in going away. I guessed it was the result of having a delightfully sinful and satisfying evening and an absolutely fabulous start to the day. I took a shower and got dressed in black skinny jeans and a lavender V-neck t-shirt.

Downstairs in the kitchen, I started a pot of coffee before searching for an appropriate breakfast. I was starving and toast wasn't going to cut it. At dinner the previous night I'd been unable to eat much of anything besides dessert. Alligator, squirrel, and octopus had been the main event. All three were things way beyond my comfort level. I'd been extremely relieved when dessert had arrived and it was normal—an apple tart with vanilla ice cream.

I drank a cup of coffee and decided after all the physical activity I needed to fortify myself, so I placed a carry-out order from Bob Evans and filled my travel mug with more coffee. After a brief search I found my purse, keys, and cell phone. I was finally ready to leave so I opened the back door and nearly ran into my brother Brandon.

"Damn. What are you doing here?" I asked.

"I'm just paying my sister a visit." He smiled.

"Well, you're going to have to come back another time. I'm on my way out."

"We need to talk," he said with no hint of a smile remaining.

I blew out a breath. I knew that tone. It meant he

wasn't going anywhere, which meant neither was I until he said whatever the heck was on his mind.

"Fine, but you have three minutes. I just ordered breakfast."

"No problem. I'll be quick. Stay away from Larson."

"That ass. He has such a big mouth," I muttered.

"I have no idea what you're talking about," Brandon said, picking at nonexistent lint.

"Why did Grant tell you about my meeting with Mr. Larson?" I asked.

"He didn't want to." Brandon shifted his weight from his left to his right foot. "I was at Flannigan's pub, enjoying a beer on my night off. Tompkins showed up all wound up. He sat down and asked why you were so damned stubborn. He called you, though I wasn't supposed to know it was you, and texted you. He sort of panicked when you didn't answer your phone."

"So, what? He spilled his guts about my dinner with Mr. Larson?"

"Yup. I have to admit, I got kind of worried myself," Brandon said.

"So what happened?"

"Thankfully, you finally texted him you were on your way home. He tore out of the bar." Brandon looked down at his feet. "I showed here about half an hour later. I saw Tompkin's car and figured it was all good."

I had a long-standing habit of keeping my personal life as far away from my family as possible. I had no desire to change that now, but it seemed Brandon knew too much for comfort for either of us.

"Look, Grant and I are just…"

Brandon covered his ears. "No. No. No, I don't want to know. I'm just worried about you. Stay away from Larson."

"He's a client," I said.

"Drop the case. The man is a killer."

"I didn't like it when Grant thought he could give me orders, and I really don't like it that you are pulling the same thing."

"I'm not letting something happen to you. Get Larson out of your life, or I'll tell the family about you and Tompkins, or maybe about your little trysts with Zack."

"What?" I shouted, feeling my face burn with embarrassment and anger.

"I'm sorry. I love you, and I'm not watching our parents bury a daughter." He spun around and walked off before my mouth and brain could cooperate to form words.

When they finally began to play nice together, the only thing I could think of was *jerk*.

I locked up and headed straight for Bob Evans. Once there, I added an order of sugar cookies. I took my breakfast and snack to the office. I sat at my desk and ate an order of home fries plus two biscuits covered in glorious sausage gravy. I finished my second cup of coffee and decided with the anger swirling around inside after my conversation with Brandon that I was a bit too caffeinated to drink any more—at least for now.

I turned on the computer and checked through fifty junk and spam emails. Only two were from clients, both promising the final payments had been mailed. I wouldn't hold my breath. After surfing the web and watching a dozen cat videos, I laid my head on my desk.

I opened my eyes and frowned. I couldn't figure out what the buzzing sound was. After a quick search I discovered it was my cell phone that had somehow found its way into my desk drawer. I picked it up and said, "Hello."

"Miss Murphy, thank goodness. I've just been going out of my mind," Mrs. Patterson said.

I couldn't believe it. I'd texted her four times the previous evening, doing my best to convince her everything would be all right. She was sure there was more going on but I didn't have the heart or the stomach to tell her that her late husband's killer was carrying his baby.

I looked up and scowled when I spotted Brandon in the doorway. He had the nerve to smirk. I assured Mrs. Patterson everything would be fine and finally, just to get her off the phone, I agreed to meet with her later that day.

"I'll see you around six. Goodbye, Mrs. Patterson," I said, and hung up.

I did my best to ignore my brother but he was determined not to let that happen.

"I know you see me," Brandon said. "You can't keep ignoring me."

I looked at his smiling face and frowned. "Go away," I said.

He held up a three-by-five index card and began waving it around. "I surrender."

"Excuse me?"

"You heard me," Brandon said.

Suspicious of a trap, I asked him why he was giving up so quickly.

"Because I remembered something."

"Good for you."

He laughed. "All right, smart-ass, listen. I remembered giving you orders or ultimatums doesn't work well. They tend to have you dig in your heels, even more determined than before to do whatever the hell it is someone is trying to prevent you from doing."

"That's not true," I lied.

"Hah. Yeah, it is. You think you know better," Brandon said.

"I usually do."

"That's debatable. My point is I know I can't stop you. So, I'm here to help you."

"No. Sorry, but that isn't happening."

"Yes, it is," Brandon said, rubbing his hand across his chin. "Listen, this guy is dangerous. You had dinner with him. You were in a limo with the guy."

"Look, we aren't dating. I'm working for him, and if he's guilty, I'll turn everything I have over to the department," I said.

Brandon walked over and sat down in one of the chairs across from me. "I know that. That's not what I'm worried about. I'm worried about you ending up in a coffin, or more likely a shallow grave somewhere."

"Wow, thanks for the vote of confidence." I tried to keep the hurt out of my voice but failed.

"You would make one hell of a cop except for

that mouth of yours and your entire lack of respect for authority."

I opened and closed my mouth several times in an attempt to mouth off to him but sadly no words came out. To my utter despair, Brandon took that as a sign to continue.

"You always end up getting yourself into the weirdest situations. How many times have you been kidnapped? I mean, who gets kidnapped? Much less more than once."

I kept my lips clamped shut. There was no way I was going to inform him of the earlier ride in Mr. Larson's limo I had been forced to participate in. I would never hear the end of it. Plus, it was possible Brandon would call our brother Michael and the two of them would discreetly dispose of Mr. Larson. They were upstanding citizens, awesome brothers—most of, or at least some of, the time— and by the book cops. They were also human, and if they truly feared for my safety or anyone else in our family, I wasn't sure exactly how far they'd go to protect us. I just sincerely hoped I never had to find out.

I knew how far I was willing to go to protect the ones I loved, but then again I wasn't the most stand up, law-abiding citizen in the world. I also made about the worst Catholic on the planet—at least according to Father Steve and Sister Agnes.

"I'm sorry I worried you, but really, I won't be meeting with him alone again. Any future meetings will be in public places that I determine," I said, hoping to allay his fears.

"That's a start. From now on I'll be attending

every meeting along with you," Brandon said.

I opened my mouth to protest but Brandon shook his head *no*.

"That is non-negotiable," he said.

"Fine," I said through clenched lips.

"See, we can get along. This could even be fun."

"Yeah, sure."

Brandon glanced down at his watch. "I've gotta get going." He tossed the index card on my desk and stood up to leave. He glanced away from me. "Could we, uh, forget about what I said earlier, I mean at your place about, uh, things."

"Absolutely."

"Thank God." He turned around. "See ya later." He practically ran out of my office.

When he was gone I sighed in relief. The last thing either of us would want to discuss was our personal lives. Yuck. I didn't want to think about some of the loser girlfriends he'd had, and I certainly didn't want to discuss my relationships or whatever they were with Brandon, or anyone for that matter.

The rest of the morning was quiet. Sadly there wasn't much for me to do except for what little paperwork was left. I spent a couple of hours finishing it up. Around noon I put my head on my desk and *accidently* fell asleep. I opened my eyes and lifted my head. According to the clock on the wall I'd napped for almost two hours. I considered my options; I could do some research on Mr. Larson's case, I could go back to sleep, or I could call it a day and head home. It didn't take long for me to decide home was exactly where I wanted to be.

I shut off the computer, watered the one plant in the corner, and locked up the office. At home, I walked into the living room and kicked off my shoes. I had plenty of time before my meeting with Mrs. Patterson at six o'clock. I flipped on the TV and was happy to find a repeat episode of *Fixer Upper* on HGTV. It was my second favorite show after *Property Brothers*. Who could pass up an opportunity to watch and drool over twins Drew and Jonathan?

Whenever I watched these shows I had a sudden urge to knock down a wall and have the whole open floor concept. Well, not knocking the wall down myself, but having someone else do it. Though I was pretty sure my apartment landlord wouldn't be too thrilled if I hired some cute contractors to knock down his walls. I was a little bummed until I remembered all the obnoxious banging noise the roofers had made while they were replacing the roof.

I looked around the room and admitted that the place could use some professional help. I was pretty sure my family would say the same thing about me, but whatever. After the episode ended I wandered into the kitchen in search of food. Since I would be driving I skipped on the beer and grabbed a can of Diet Coke out of the fridge. I made a turkey sandwich with lettuce, tomato, mayonnaise, and two strips of bacon on white bread. I added a bag of Cool Ranch Doritos and headed back to the living room just in time for an episode of *Love It or List It*.

The two of them bickered like an old married

couple, which was probably why I enjoyed the show so much. After my dinner was finished I dug out the bag of cookies from my purse and voilà, dessert was ready.

My cell phone began to ring. By the time I dug it out of the bottom of my purse, I'd missed the call. Normally, I wasn't thrilled to miss a call, but this time I was extremely happy. Not having to deal with the annoying reporter, Mr. Abraham, was just fine by me. Of course, when I didn't answer the cell phone, my home phone began to ring. I didn't think it was a coincidence so I let the machine get it. Sure enough, I could hear his annoying, condescending voice asking me to return his calls. Yeah, that'd be the day I decide to shave off all my hair and move to the wilds of Alaska.

I cleaned up the few dishes I'd used for dinner and headed upstairs. After a quick stop in the bathroom and a quick wave of the mascara wand I figured I was ready to get this over with. I truly felt for Mrs. Patterson but I didn't have enough emotional stability of my own to be lending any to someone else.

I scooped up my purse from the couch and walked to the back door. I opened it and practically snarled. Standing on my porch with a microphone in his hand and a cameraman behind him was the annoying Mr. Abraham in the flesh.

"Go away," I said.

"Don't you want to comment about your client, Mr. Larson?" he asked, smiling and shoving the microphone mere inches from my face.

"What are you talking about?" I asked.

"I had an interview with your new client, Mr. Larson. He claims you believe in his innocence and are working hard to find the real killer." He smirked before asking if I'd care to comment.

"No, I wouldn't. Now get lost. You're trespassing on private property."

"If I were working for a suspected murderer, I might want to explain myself," Mr. Abraham said.

"I don't owe anyone an explanation," I said through gritted teeth.

"Maybe not to our viewers, but what about the victim's family? Don't they deserve some answers?" He smiled when the cameraman came in for a close up.

"Yes, *they* do, but *you* don't. Now, get away from me before I call the cops," I said.

Mr. Abraham waved his hand across his throat and the cameraman shut off the camera and pointed it away from me. "How about speaking off the record?" he asked.

"No." I walked past him and got into my car without looking back. I pulled out of the parking lot and sped off, so even if he wanted to follow me, he couldn't. I pulled into the Pattersons' driveway and parked behind a white Porsche. I got out of my car and walked up the walkway to the front door. I rang the bell and waited.

Mrs. Patterson opened the door. Her face was flushed and naked of any makeup. Her hair, pulled back into a ponytail, was messy with hairs escaping from it in all different directions. Mrs. Patterson's clothes were wrinkled and looked like she'd slept in them. She tried to smile but it resembled a grimace.

"Miss Murphy, please come in." Mrs. Patterson stepped aside.

I walked past her and she quickly closed the door. I followed her toward the kitchen but instead she led us toward the living room where I was surprised to find Mrs. Tipton sitting on the couch, holding a half-empty glass of wine and wearing enough jewelry to be seen from the International Space Station. Her hair was neatly swept back and up off her neck. Her wrap dress was a bit too red and way too tight. I also had an unobstructed view of absolutely way too much cleavage. I feared if she had a wardrobe malfunction, she might take out Mrs. Patterson and myself. Scary.

"Miss Murphy, it's so nice of you to come over here and reassure Shaina." Mrs. Tipton's smile didn't reveal any teeth.

"It's no trouble," I said.

Mrs. Patterson motioned for me to have a seat. I chose a chair across from the couch.

"Would you like some wine?" Mrs. Tipton asked.

"No, thanks," I said, thinking it odd she would offer me a drink as, like me, she was a guest in this home. Though I wasn't sure if she'd been invited or simply invited herself. I couldn't imagine these two women wanting to spend any time together.

I turned toward Mrs. Patterson, who had taken a seat on the couch. She reached for her own half-empty glass of wine. "So, how are you feeling?" I asked.

"Fine," she said before taking a rather large drink from her glass.

"Slow down there, Shaina. You don't want to get sloshed," Mrs. Tipton said.

I watched as Mrs. Patterson placed the glass back on the coffee table, her hands trembling.

"So, what can I do for you?" I asked.

"Well, we were just so relieved to hear the real killer was caught," Mrs. Tipton replied. "I never believed that old lady had anything to do with it."

I was sure Aunt Tessa wouldn't appreciate the old lady part but would enjoy the presumed innocent part.

"Yes, well, it seems to have all worked out," I said for lack anything else to say.

"I agree," said Mrs. Tipton.

Mrs. Patterson looked at Mrs. Tipton before looking back at me and nodding. This whole thing was weird.

"So, is there anything I can do?" I asked, eager to find out why I was here and to get the hell out. I wasn't sure how either of them could stand to be in the same room together.

"I thought—"

"Shaina was wondering if there was any chance that redheaded hussy could be released," Mrs. Tipton said, cutting off Mrs. Patterson.

"The odds of her getting bail are slim. If you'd like, you could talk with the investigator in charge or the district attorney's office," I said.

"Ooh, that hot cop. I wouldn't mind getting some one-on-one time with him." Mrs. Tipton laughed. "He could frisk me any time. What about you?" She elbowed Mrs. Patterson in the ribs.

"I think I'll pass."

227

I was unprepared for the amount of jealousy that shot through me. The woman had no idea she was talking about Grant. The man I...well, I liked him a lot, but I wasn't sure if it was love. I didn't think I'd ever be ready for that again.

I bit my lower lip in a desperate attempt to keep from saying anything that even remotely sounded like a jealous lover. Fortunately, the two of them seemed unaware of my discomfort.

"Do you have any idea why she killed poor Derek?" Mrs. Tipton asked.

I glanced at Mrs. Patterson and frowned. I had been avoiding this but I wasn't sure for how much longer I'd be able to get away with it.

"I'm not sure," I said.

"Oh, come on, you have to have some idea." Mrs. Tipton pointed to Mrs. Patterson. "Don't you think she should know the truth?"

I hesitated but finally decided to just spill it. She would eventually find out and, well, maybe if she learned the truth, Mrs. Patterson could begin to move on with her life.

I straightened my posture and looked Mrs. Patterson square in the eyes. "It would appear your husband's lover was pregnant," I said.

Mrs. Patterson looked toward Mrs. Tipton before looking back at me. "What?"

"I'm sorry. She's pregnant. I guess they fought over his lack of interest in leaving you for her and their baby. Though she claims he was going to do just that."

"This is insane," Mrs. Patterson said.

"There's no way he would have left Shaina. I

would know," Mrs. Tipton said.

I didn't think Mrs. Patterson could take one more shock at the moment. Though to be honest she didn't seem all that upset. I was pretty sure if I'd just been told my dead ex was going to be a father, I'd have been swearing enough to make the entire Navy blush, but maybe that was just me.

"Yes, well, I guess that's why Miss Greer killed him."

"Excellent. Now I think it's time for a celebration," Mrs. Tipton said, picking up her glass and downing what was left inside.

"Excuse me?" I asked, convinced I'd heard her wrong.

"That slutty home-wrecker is going to finally get what she deserves." She smiled. "Isn't that a reason to celebrate?"

I glanced at Mrs. Patterson. She didn't look too convinced now was a time to party. In fact, she looked as if she was about to toss her cookies. I sincerely hoped she didn't because I'd end up tossing my dinner also.

"Maybe now isn't the best time," I said, hoping Mrs. Tipton would take a hint.

"Nonsense. Of course now is a good time." She refilled her glass before pouring more wine into Mrs. Patterson's glass. She then poured some into an empty glass and handed it to me.

I tried to politely decline but Mrs. Tipton was having none of it. I lifted the glass, determined to take a single sip from the glass before making my excuses and escaping from here and never ever returning again.

CHAPTER TWELVE

I opened my eyes. At least I thought I had, but it was so dark I couldn't be sure. My head felt weird and my tongue felt like it had suddenly doubled in size. I had no idea what was going on but it was most assuredly a sign I'd had way too much to drink. It was funny because I couldn't remember drinking a lot, but then again I couldn't remember much of anything.

I tried to move my legs but couldn't. I also was struggling to keep my eyes open. After several attempts I gave up the battle. I curled up on the lumpy surface and fell back asleep.

The next time I opened my eyes I wished I'd kept them closed. Besides discovering I was on a cold, damp floor, there was also the realization my head hurt like hell. There was a small speck of light that seemed to be off in the distance.

There was a rancid smell I was almost positive wasn't coming from me. I tried to sit up but my body wouldn't cooperate. As I kept trying I came to the horribly terrifying realization my arms were tied together somehow. I tried to move my legs but they moved as one.

This was so not good. I took several deep breaths, letting each one out slowly. The last thing I needed to do was panic. That was easily thought but not so easy to pull off. The good news was my hands were in front of me. That meant I had a chance to work on whatever was binding my feet together.

After too many failed attempts to count I made it to an upright position. I leaned back against a wall and sighed. I did some more breathing—extremely pleased I still could, considering the situation— before getting to work on the binds around my ankles. A task made all the more difficult with my hands tied together and the miniscule amount of light entering the room.

I felt around, searching for a knot. This was going to be a bitch. Undoing knots was tricky business, but doing it half blind meant I'd be lucky if I finished in anything under forty-eight hours. I was pretty sure whoever had drugged me and tossed me inside this place wasn't planning on keeping me around that long.

That thought was incentive enough to get me moving, but a sound to my right had me freezing in place. I sat as still as possible. I held my breath and waited. A few seconds later I heard the noise again. I couldn't tell what it was but I had a sudden overwhelming feeling I wasn't alone.

The first thought that came to mind was something creepy and crawly and disgusting. I shook my head and tried to empty it of all thoughts of snakes, rodents, and, I shivered, arachnids. If I was going to get out of here, I needed a clear head, and focusing on some of my most immense fears would be a distraction that could very well get me killed—yet another cheery thought.

Doing my best to ignore the noises emanating just a few feet from me, I got to work on removing my restraints and freeing my legs. I was making real progress, at least I thought so, when the muffled sounds seemed to be taking shape into words.

"Oh God, my head," Mrs. Patterson said.

I almost cried out in my relief to know that the creepy thing in the dark was another human. Though that may not be as reassuring as it should be since the last memory I had was of having a drink with her and Mrs. Tipton. I was tempted to remain silent and see what happened but my curiosity and concern for my fellow human captive won out.

"Are you all right?" I asked.

"I don't know. Miss Murphy, is that you?" Mrs. Patterson asked.

"Yes, it's me. What the hell happened?"

For a moment there was nothing but the sound of our breathing. Just when I thought she'd lost consciousness she responded.

"I'm not sure."

"What's the last thing you remember?" I asked.

After another long pause she spoke. "Helping Tanya tie your hands," she said.

I gasped. "What the hell?"

"I'm so sorry. You were never supposed to get hurt. No one was." She sighed. "Well, nobody besides Derek."

"You murdered your husband?"

"I—"

"Wait. Don't answer that. Right now, all I care about is why we are in here and how the hell do we get out?"

"This is an abandoned house. It's where we, um, took care of Derek."

"Okay, so how do we get out of here? Wait, are you tied up?" I asked.

I could hear her moving around, testing out her bounds. "Nope."

"Great. Now please get over here and help me."

After a minute or so I felt her hand on my shoulder. At least I prayed it was hers.

"What can I do?" she asked.

"For starters, you can untie my feet. Then my hands."

I sat as still as possible over the next several minutes. Instead of lashing out I bit my tongue. I was afraid if I kept that up I'd need plastic surgery to repair the damage. On the plus side I could end up with lips like Angelina Jolie. Actually, that might be another negative. Yikes.

After days of torture that only lasted mere minutes my legs were free and I was so happy to be able to move them. I tried to stand up, landing on my butt for the effort. I smacked my forehead. I should have remembered from the last time I'd been trussed up like a Thanksgiving dinner it would take a few minutes for the feeling to return to my legs.

I had her start on the bindings around my wrists. While I waited for Mrs. Patterson to finish, I pressed her for answers—at least the ones I needed to get us out of here. I started firing questions at her. "How many exits are there? What floor are we on? Is Tanya armed? Where's my purse?"

"We're on the second floor. There are a few doors and windows," Mrs. Patterson replied.

"What about weapons? Does she have any? Did she look in my purse?"

"I'm almost positive she has a gun. I don't know where your purse is. For all I know she left it at my house."

That might be good. I hoped someone in my family had figured out I was missing and was currently doing everything they could to find me. Since I couldn't count on that, the only person I could rely on to get me out of this mess was me. With a final tug my hands were free. I thanked her before asking her to help me up.

With her assistance I was able to stand. I leaned on her and we shuffled our way across the room toward the small opening with light shining through. I reached up and yanked the fabric down that had been shielding us from the sun.

I squinted and turned my head to protect myself from the intensity. I had no idea how long we stood there averting our eyes, but eventually we both turned back toward the window.

Overgrown yards and boarded up buildings stood in single file lines on either side of the street. Tanya would have all the privacy she needed to dispose of two nuisances. Mrs. Patterson had been right when she'd said we were on the second floor. Not an enormous fan of heights, I wasn't eager to go out the window, but if it meant staying alive, I was willing to do it.

I looked around the now sun filled room to see if there was anything inside we could use to aid us in our escape. The only things inside the small former bedroom were a rocking chair, a floor lamp in the corner, and a folded up tarp. The thought of the tarp's purpose had my stomach roiling.

I looked away and got a clear look at Mrs. Patterson. She had dark smudges on her face and her lipstick was smeared. Her eyes were bloodshot.

"We need to get out of here," she said.

I agreed. I looked over at the door. Maybe, if we were lucky, Tanya had forgotten to lock it. I walked over to the door and reached for the handle just as it began to turn. I wasn't sure who was more surprised, me or Tanya, when we were suddenly standing face to face. I moved to shove her out of the way but froze when I spotted the gun pointed at my chest.

"Back up," Tanya said.

I stood my ground, desperate to keep her out of the room. If I could lock her out, the delay could give Mrs. Patterson and me enough time to escape through the window and head for help.

"I said move back or your visit to the Golden Gates is going to get here sooner than I had planned."

"Why is she going to McDonald's? Doesn't she know fast food isn't good for you?" Mrs. Patterson asked. Shocked, Tanya and I both turned to look at Mrs. Patterson. "What?" she asked.

I turned back toward Tanya and noticed the gun was no longer pointed directly at me. That could be my chance. Without thinking, I shoved Tanya backward and closed the door. It was my bad luck I hadn't noticed the lock on this side of the door no longer worked.

Tanya shouted and started banging on the door. There was nothing we could use to shove in front of the door to keep her out. I yelled at Mrs. Patterson to break the window as I threw my body against the door. I leaned against it and prayed she wouldn't fire into the door. If she did, I most assuredly would be done for, and while Tanya had suggested I'd be headed toward Saint Peter, I was pretty sure I would be heading somewhere a little south of there. Someplace that would require the material NASA used on their space shuttles to prevent them from burning up on reentry.

I risked a glance over at Mrs. Patterson and found her trying to force the window open. I shouted for her to break it. That slight loss in concentration was enough to have me thrown forward and Tanya took full advantage, charging into the room.

"Get the hell away from that window!" Tanya shouted.

"You need to let us out of here," Mrs. Patterson said, taking a few steps to her right.

"Oh, you'll both be leaving, but not yet." Tanya glanced at the tarp as a little reminder of just how she planned on getting us out of here.

"Why are you doing this?" I asked.

Tanya's face turned back toward me. "You just couldn't leave it alone, could you?"

"What are you talking about?" I asked.

"I swear I've been dealing with idiots all around me. I don't understand it," Tanya said, ignoring my question.

"I said I was sorry a dozen times. What else did you want me to do?" Mrs. Patterson asked.

"Not only did you mix up the houses, twice, you kept moving the body. What the hell was wrong with you?" She kept on without waiting for a response. "Then you couldn't even play the grieving widow correctly. You got this one here suspicious," Tanya said, pointing the gun in my direction for emphasis.

"I have no idea what you're talking about," I said, stalling for time to come up with a plan.

"Oh, yes, you do. How many times did you visit that little slut?" Tanya asked.

"I wasn't visiting her. I was questioning her," I replied.

"Yeah, sure, but somehow she managed to get her claws in you too."

"What are you talking about?" I asked, honestly perplexed.

"I know she called you. She wanted your help."

"How do you—"

"I slept with her lawyer. He's been a friend of my husband's for years," Tanya said.

"I still don't understand what any of this has to do with me," I said, glancing over at Mrs. Patterson. She was swaying side to side. I feared she'd tip over. Though it could be just the distraction I needed.

"I had this all planned out. That bitch thought she'd sweep in and take Derek away from us? No way. We killed him and set her up to take the fall, but thanks to this one's incompetence, that got all screwed up."

"I'm sorry, but all those houses look alike and the names were just crazy." Mrs. Patterson put her hand to her head. "My head hurts."

"Don't worry, it won't for much longer."

Tanya's smile sent a shiver up and down my spine.

"You don't have to do this," I said.

"I really need some aspirin," Mrs. Patterson said, taking several steps toward Tanya.

"Don't move," Tanya said, turning away from me.

With all of her attention focused on Mrs. Patterson, I figured now was my chance. I grabbed the floor lamp, spun around, and swung the lamp as hard as I could, hitting Tanya in the back. As she fell forward the gun went off. I looked over to see Mrs. Patterson slump down to the floor.

Tanya started screaming and cussing as she tried to stand up. I dove to the ground and landed on her. I tried to reach for the gun and the two of us struggled. Tanya elbowed me in the eye and I pulled her hair. It was a girl move but I didn't care. After several moments of struggling I finally wrestled the gun from her. I rolled away from her. I sat up and pointed the gun at her chest. Between panting breaths I warned her not to move.

"You ruined everything!"

I chanced a look around and spotted Mrs. Patterson sitting up, holding her hands against the left side of her head with what looked like blood trickling down her arm.

"I'm sorry. I did everything you told me to do. I even pretended to need Miss Murphy's help. What else did you want from me?"

"How about some competency? Was that too much to ask?" Tanya spat.

"Thanks for that," I said, annoyed for some peculiar reason.

"I'm sorry, Miss Murphy. I didn't mean it like that," Mrs. Patterson said.

"Uh-huh."

"Seriously, at first I was pretending, but then you were so kind to me that I started to think of you as a real friend."

Unconvinced, I shook my head. "Whatever," I said.

"We can fix this," Mrs. Patterson said.

"How? You fool, she has the gun."

"What if we offer her money?" Mrs. Patterson turned toward me. "What if I gave you twenty thousand dollars from Derek's estate? Would you let us go?"

I couldn't believe she was honestly asking me to let two killers go for ten thousand each. These women were crazy, like batshit crazy, and needed to be locked up for life.

"Look at her. She isn't going to forget I tried to kill her," Tanya said.

What she didn't say was that it appeared Mrs. Patterson had already seemed to have forgotten Tanya's latest plan had included killing her off as well. Jeez, they'd killed Derek for his lack of ability to be faithful, yet the two of them couldn't stay loyal to each other long enough to get away with it. For that I was grateful. If she'd been successful, I could have ended up as dead as Derek.

I needed to get help. These two needed to be locked up. I asked Tanya where my phone was and her response was telling me to find it myself.

"Damn it, where is it?" I asked.

"Go to Hell," Tanya replied.

I eased myself up and took several steps toward the door. I turned slightly to grab the doorknob. Tanya pounced. She grabbed my ankle and yanked. I tried to kick her but lost my balance and fell to the floor.

Tanya grabbed for the gun. I knew if she took it, I was dead. I shouted for her to stop but she ignored me, her hand clasping my wrist. I squeezed the trigger. Tanya froze then looked at me in horror. Her face quickly contorted back to anger, and despite her injury, tried to wrench the gun from my hand. I squeezed the trigger three more times.

Tanya collapsed into a heap on the floor. I turned away from the sight of the blood pooling around her. The sound of the gun firing echoed over and over in my head. I tried to take slow, deep breaths but felt like I was gasping for air.

"Oh my God. You killed her!" Mrs. Patterson shouted.

Ignoring her, I turned away and yanked the door open. I searched the house for any signs of a phone. Eventually I found my car in the garage. I could see my purse on the passenger's seat. I opened the door, dug into my purse, and found my phone.

Almost on auto pilot I called 911 and reported

my emergency. I hung up and dialed Grant's number.

"Where the hell are you?" he asked. "We've been looking for you for hours."

"I just killed one of Derek Patterson's killers. The other one is somewhere inside the house."

"What? Where are you?"

"I've gotta go. I'm gonna be sick." I raced out the garage door and bent at the waist. I emptied what little food I'd had. I'd forgotten to hang up the phone and once the wrenching was over I could still hear Grant shouting into the phone. Luckily I didn't have to respond to him because several patrol cars raced up to the house.

I took several steps away from the house and placed the gun on the driveway before collapsing into a pair of muscular arms.

***

I woke up in the back of an ambulance. My mother was sitting to my left while my father stood outside at the rear of the vehicle. Their faces were grim. I was sure once I'd fully recovered I was in for the lecture of all lectures about worrying my family and endangering myself. That was fine. I could take it. Later, much later.

Despite my protests I was taken to the hospital to get checked out. It turned out I'd been drugged. According to Mrs. Patterson, Tanya had slipped the drug into my glass of wine. Other than the loud ringing in my ears and the fact I'd been drugged, I was eventually given a clean bill of health and released.

Despite my mother's urging I chose to go home to my own apartment. Once there, my mother refused to leave. My father didn't even try to convince her not to stay. He knew that was a battle he couldn't win. He gave me a kiss on the forehead and told me he'd be back tomorrow to check on me. My mom walked him to the door. They said goodbyes in hushed tones before a hug and kisses that would embarrass the hell out of any teenager catching their parents showing any signs of affection. I was just grateful they weren't arguing over me.

My mom tucked me in on the couch. I spent the next several hours in a fitful sleep. It seemed taking a life wasn't conducive to a restful night's sleep. It didn't matter that the woman had been batshit crazy or that she'd already killed one person, framed another, and was about to commit a double homicide.

Over the next twenty-four hours I had numerous visitors. My mother made sure the visits were short, though some like Melissa, Shandra, and Charmaine got a little extra time, what with being my best friends and all. Plus, they'd brought all kinds of goodies; donuts, paperback books, and enough Chinese takeout and pizza to feed all of us for a week.

Grant and Zack had both shown up. My mom had made herself scarce during their visits. Zack had brought a dozen yellow roses, my favorite, with a single red one in the center. He'd kissed me on the lips and made me promise not to do anything foolish again. When he'd gotten up to leave I'd so wanted to ask him to stay, but I smiled and waved goodbye instead.

Grant had shown up with a copy of my signed statement I'd made while at the hospital. Since Mrs. Patterson's statement had been similar to mine, it looked like I was in the clear, at least legally, for killing Tanya Tipton.

Grant sat across from me. "How are you doing?" he asked.

"Fine. I guess."

"You had us scared pretty good." Grant ran his hands through his hair.

"Sorry."

"I'm pretty sure I'm going to have a complaint in my file."

A sickening feeling hit my stomach. "What did you do?" I asked, unsure if I even wanted the answer.

"I kind of had words with Mr. Larson."

"Oh jeez, Grant, what the hell were you thinking?"

"You were missing. I wasn't thinking. I was out of my fucking mind!"

"Don't worry. I'll call him and smooth things over."

"I wish you wouldn't, but I know there's no point in me asking. You're going to do whatever the hell you want."

"Hey, do you mind? I almost died. You could be a little sympathetic."

Grant jumped up from the chair and pointed at me. "You drive me insane."

"That's not my fault."

He turned away so I couldn't see his face. "I don't want anything to happen to you."

"Why?" I whispered.

He turned back toward me. His eyes looked over my face. "Do you really not know?" he asked.

Blood rushed to my face, causing my skin to burn.

"I love the way your nose crinkles like that whenever you're embarrassed."

"Shut up," I said.

Grant laughed. "So, how long can I stay before your mom kicks me out?"

"I figure you've got a while. I'm sure she's upstairs pretending to not know what's going on down here," I said.

"Good." Grant walked over and kneeled in front of me. He took my hands in his. "I care about you. And the thought of losing you is not something I ever want to go through again."

"I'm sorry you were worried."

"Me too."

I scooched over, making room on the couch.

"Are you going to share those donuts?" he asked.

"Maybe. What do I get in return?"

Grant smiled, leaned over, and whispered some absolutely lovely things he intended to do once I was no longer on house arrest from my mom.

Yay.

"Well, Mrs. Patterson will be indicted for murder and one count of attempted murder."

I closed my eyes. If only shutting out the horror could be as easy.

ABOUT THE AUTHOR

Growing up Violet Ingram spent Saturday mornings in the library. Her first literary loves were Hardy Boys, Nancy Drew, and Encyclopedia Brown. She always imagined herself helping solve the mysteries.

Violet dreamed of being a singer, a world famous movie star, a veterinarian, and a marine biologist. Turns out she can't sing, is a homebody, squeamish at the sight of blood, and can't swim.

After becoming a stay-at-home mom, she dreamed of turning her hobby of writing stories into a career. With the support of her family and friends, this dream became a reality.

Violet lives in the Midwest where she is busy keeping up with her hubby, their 5 kids, and glued to her computer putting the scenes in her head onto the screen.

Facebook:

https://www.facebook.com/violet.ingram.39?ref=bookmarks

Twitter:

https://twitter.com/violetingram

Blog:

http://violetingram.blogspot.com/